The Emerald Collar

(An Eden Twins Mystery)

Penelope J. McDonald

The Emerald Collar (An Eden Twins Mystery)
By Penelope J. McDonald
Copyright 2015 Penelope J. McDonald

Published by Penelope J. McDonald
Printed and bound in the United States of America
ISBN: 13:978-1514243527
ISBN: 10:1514243520

Cover design by **Ares Jun**
Formatting and layout provided by **Quantum Formatting Service**

DEDICATION

Dedicated to the memory of Jill Mallett—my mother, my teacher, my friend—who first read me a story, and Leslie Mallett, my father, who bought me a typewriter so that I could write my own.

CHAPTER ONE

NORTH VANCOUVER, BRITISH COLUMBIA
Summer, 1951

Alice grinned like a Cheshire cat when she peered through a gated opening in the laurel hedge with her sister, Emma and their dog, Murphy. "It's a castle, just like I imagined. There's a turret with a telescope, and a whale weathervane on the roof," she shrieked. With nimble fingers the twins unfastened the anchor-shaped latch on the twisted wire gate and bolted up the pathway leading to their quirky new home.

"It looks spooky with those black storm clouds swirling overhead and the weathervane squeaking in the wind," said Emma, her voice trailing off as she eyed the mansion towering before them. "The colour of the front stairs is kind of creepy too. Blood red—yuck! Maybe there's a ghost living here."

"Well, girls, what do you think?" asked their father, who trudged up the path with luggage from the trunk of the car while their mother carried an armful of blankets. "You can get lost in this house it's so big and there's an enormous garden to run around in. Just think of the fun you'll have exploring." He ascended the stairs and dropped the suitcases at the front entrance. "Let's see what's inside."

The twins watched with anticipation as their father took a large brass key from his pocket, undid the lock and opened the heavy front door. The telltale smell of old wood and polished hardwood floors escaped from the home and enveloped them. They wrinkled their noses and stared in awe at the grandeur of their new surroundings.

"Wow," said Alice when she stepped inside and noticed a sparkling chandelier hanging overhead. When she looked down the long hallway she counted five glass doors opening into immense rooms decorated with unusual artwork on the walls. Two rooms featured massive stone fireplaces with decorative clam shells carved into chunky cedar mantlepieces.

"This place is very fancy," said Emma. "It looks like a grand palace. Even the door knobs are chiseled from glass. And look, there's a telephone on the wall. We've always wanted a telephone."

At the end of the hallway the girls stopped and stared at a winding staircase which curled around the corner out of sight. "I wonder what's upstairs," said Emma, her eyes flashing.

Alice giggled. "I have an eerie feeling that a ghost wants us to climb the stairs and find out."

Before they set foot on the shiny black steps, Murphy rushed past the girls, tore up the stairs and disappeared. Alice and Emma chased after him. When they reached the landing where a little window overlooked the back yard, they turned and climbed the last few steps to the top floor where three bedrooms and a lavish bathroom with a claw-foot bathtub awaited. Murphy was nowhere to be seen. Suddenly, they heard him whining. They followed the noise and found him sitting, tail wagging, in front of a little doorway hidden in one of the closets. When the girls yanked the door open they squealed with delight. Murphy had sniffed out the worn steps leading to the turret.

Driving rain from a summer thunderstorm pelted the windows throughout the night. The twins found it impossible to sleep. Each time the lightning flashed, Alice and Emma saw ghoulish faces staring at them through the twisted ivy leaves and arbour pattern on the wallpaper surrounding their bedroom. They screeched and yanked the blankets over their heads and imagined the creatures leaping from the walls to attack them. Early the next morning when they pulled back the curtains to find a dark, damp day, they noticed a bone glistening on the wet grass beneath their bedroom window.

"Let's sneak outside and have a look at it before Mum and Dad get up," Alice said quietly while she put a raincoat on over her pyjamas and stepped into her gum boots.

"Are you sure it's a bone? I've never seen one that big," Emma's voice trembled with excitement.

"Yes. Hurry."

Emma grabbed her jacket and put her boots on, almost tripping over Murphy who rushed past her to follow Alice out the front door.

The bone, unlike any of the round ones their

4

mother boiled up for Murphy to chew on, was big and long. "It's freaky," Emma squawked. She clutched Alice's hand and shivered in the drizzling rain. "Do you think it's part of somebody's leg?"

Alice shuddered, and buckled up her raincoat. "Ugh. What a thought. I don't know, but whatever it is, it's scary. I had a funny feeling about this place when I first saw it too. Maybe there really *is* a ghost living here."

For a moment, the twins stood wide-eyed and stared at the thing before they moved closer and bent down for a better look. All of a sudden, Murphy pushed the bone with his nose and started to whimper, prompting Emma to jump up and kick it away with her foot. "What should we do, Alice?"

"Let's get Murphy to sniff around and see if he can find any more. Beagles have a keen sense of smell."

"But he's not a real beagle," argued Emma.

Alice looked at the tri-coloured undersized hound with his too-small ears and black gumdrop nose and gave him a hug. "He was supposed to be a beagle. I know he's not a purebred. But, it doesn't matter. Murphy's got a good nose and that's what counts. Maybe a skeleton is lying in the garden. I'll run and get a shovel. You get Murphy to check everything out. If he gets excited, we'll know where to dig."

When Alice returned, Murphy was eagerly pawing the dirt near a big rose bush. "Start digging here, Murphy's been going crazy," said Emma as the misty rain continued to fall from the heavily overcast sky.

Alice dug the shovel into the ground and worked as fast as she could. Suddenly, it hit something hard. "Let's see what it is." Alice put her hand into the hole and pulled out a hard lump. She shook the dirt off, and then put it on the grass.

"Phooey," said Emma. "It's just one of Murphy's dog bones. Let's bury it again. We can't leave a hole in the garden, and we don't want Mum and Dad to see anything suspicious."

"That's for sure." Alice threw it back into the hole, covered it with earth, and then ran with the shovel back to the shed.

"What are we going to do with this long bone?" Emma asked when Alice returned. "Maybe we should bury it too. Or, show it to Mum and Dad."

Alice put her hands on her hips and frowned.

"Why? We don't know what it is or where it came from. We've always wanted a mystery to solve and here's one staring us in the face. Think of it as an adventure. It's our chance to become real detectives. Don't you find that exciting?"

"Yes, but …," Emma began.

"Don't worry. We'll clean it up and hide it on the top shelf in our cupboard. Mum and Dad mustn't know what we've been up to."

"Oh, no!" Emma squealed. "The light's on in their bedroom. Let's get inside quick."

Alice grabbed the bone, and the three of them dashed into the house. "The bone will be our secret. We've got to solve this puzzle," said Alice quietly. "If Nancy Drew can do it, so can we."

"That was quite a storm last night. We heard you scream," said their mother at breakfast. "When I peeked in your room to check on you both, you were asleep under the covers with Murphy. Or were you just pretending? The thunder was awfully loud."

Emma spoke first. "We were hiding under the

blankets because we were scared."

"Really scared!" said Alice. "It wasn't the thunder. It was the creepy faces staring at us from the wallpaper. They were hiding behind the ivy and we thought they were coming to get us. Every time the lightning flashed we saw them, so we ducked under the covers."

When the twins examined the wallpaper with their mother, no one could see any frightening faces. "Maybe they only come out during thunderstorms when lightning strikes," Emma suggested.

Mum squinted and shook her head. "Well there's nothing here but ivy now."

"We're not kidding. They were there, and they looked real," continued Emma.

Alice nodded in agreement. "She's telling the truth, honestly."

"You girls do have vivid imaginations. I'll speak to your father and see if we can change the wallpaper one of these days. I'm sure we can find something that won't give you nightmares."

"That's a really good idea. Thanks, Mum," the twins chimed, and then skipped happily out of the bedroom and down the stairs, relieved that their bone caper was safe.

CHAPTER TWO

I had my doubts about this place, but I really like it now. It's not as scary as I first thought," Emma said, thinking about the overnight thunderstorm and the bone they found. "I love the secret places where we can hide and spy on everyone."

"I do too," said Alice. "The hiding spot under the front stairs is the best. And the turret with its neat stuff is going to be lots of fun. I've never seen Murphy so happy." She giggled and ruffled his fur. "I wonder what's going to happen next."

Two days after the twins discovered the strange bone, Murphy found another and carried it into the house at suppertime. When he dropped it on the kitchen floor, the twins gasped, and watched in disbelief when their father rose from his chair and picked it up.

"Good heavens. That's not a leg bone is it?" Mum asked in a quivering voice.

"Looks like it could be," said Dad, setting the bone on a piece of newspaper on the counter, away from Murphy who was jumping up and down trying to get it.

When their father went to wash his hands, Emma kicked Alice underneath the dinner table and whispered in her ear. "It looks exactly like ours."

"I know. This is crazy," Alice replied quietly.

Mum frowned and looked quizzically at her husband. "Do you think it's human? Perhaps we jumped too fast when we purchased this property. Maybe something bad happened here. I'm worried."

"Don't fret," Dad said, struggling to keep his concern in check. "I'm sure there's a simple answer. Perhaps someone threw it over the hedge as a joke. Maybe Murphy found it down the lane and brought it home. It may not be human. I'll call the police first thing tomorrow and let them handle the situation."

"We'll take Murphy upstairs to settle him down," Alice offered, not wanting to join in the conversation with their parents. She and Emma had a quick look at the dusty bone, then raced Murphy to their bedroom.

"Wow. Now we have a *real* mystery," Alice giggled when she stood on her toes and pushed a box aside to check the back of a shelf where their bone was hidden. "It's still here, Emma. Thank goodness."

"Mum and Dad would sure be surprised if they knew we had already found one identical to this. Should we show it to them now?" Emma asked.

"Not yet," Alice answered. "Let's leave it here. I have a strange feeling that a lot more bones are going to show up." She snickered, and when she looked at Emma, both of them tumbled onto the bed in fits of laughter.

CHAPTER THREE

The next day the twins were up early. They couldn't wait until the police arrived. "Let's hide and watch for them," suggested Alice.

"Perfect," said Emma. Murphy followed the girls when they grabbed a blanket from their closet and charged downstairs to the basement where they opened a creaky little wooden door leading to a small storage area beneath the front stairs. A dim light bulb in the doorway revealed an array of cobwebs hanging from narrow shelves, and odds and ends tacked to both walls of the staircase. Emma shuddered when she spied the cobwebs.

"You know how scared I am of spiders." She screamed when she saw a big one crawling out of the woodwork.

Alice wasn't afraid of spiders and tried to calm her sister. "It will be okay. We'll get Murphy to stomp on them." She brushed the spider from the wall, then looked at Murphy and pointed. "Get him, boy. Get him." Murphy jumped on the spider with both front feet and ground it into the dirt, all the while barking and wagging his tail. "See? Nothing to worry about."

"Thank you," Emma squeaked as she helped Alice spread the blanket on the soft earth, away from the spiders. They sat down with Murphy, peered through the cracks between the steps and waited.

When a police car arrived a short time later the twins were ready. "Here they come. Lie down, Murphy. No whining or barking," Alice ordered, and patted the dog fondly on the top of his head. "Let's listen to what they say." The girls sat silently as two police officers opened the gate and walked toward the stairs.

"What do they look like?" asked Alice.

Emma whispered, "All I can see is polished boots. It's too hard looking through the cracks. Can you see if they have guns?"

"No," answered Alice. "We'll have to wait until we get in the house. This is so exciting."

"So, a dog's found a bone. No skeleton, just an

old bone," said the officer with a deep and serious-sounding voice. "If you ask me this call is just a waste of time. I can't find anything on the books for this address," he grunted, climbing the stairs.

"If they're new here maybe they're just being cautious. Let's take a quick look at what they've got, and then be on our way," said the other officer in a more casual tone as he gawked at the mansion. "This is quite the place. Take a look at that big whale weather vane and the outlook perched on the roof. You don't see that every day. It looks just like a turret on a medieval castle where archers watched for the enemy. I bet you can see a lot of things from way up there."

"They didn't talk about murder," said Emma when the men reached the front entrance and twirled the brass doorbell. Moments later, their parents opened the door. After producing their badges and introducing themselves as Constables P.J. Avery and Len Sullivan, the policemen were ushered into the home.

Alice jumped up. "Let's go out the basement door and run around the back and see what we can find out."

As the men were led toward the kitchen where

the bone was, the twins snuck in the back door, and tiptoed into the hallway.

"Ah, there you are, girls," said their mother. "Constables Avery and Sullivan are here to look at the bone."

Alice nudged Emma who gave her sister a sideways nod when they saw the officers' holstered guns. Usually chatty, all the twins could say was a shy "Hello," when they met the officers face to face.

"Impressive," commented Avery when he glanced at the unique artwork in the rooms off the hallway. "No wonder you bought the place. It's like a museum. Just look at the painting of that huge bird." The striking oil painting of an albatross with its unbelievable 11-foot wingspread covered the entire wall of the music room.

"It's an albatross," said Alice, regaining her confidence. "They're the biggest bird on the ocean. If you look closely you can see its eyes follow you around the room. Our grandmother told us when that happens it's a sure sign that a trained artist painted the picture."

The constables raised their eyebrows and looked at the twins. "Well, it looks like you'll be learning a lot of interesting things in this house," Avery said.

"If he only knew," Alice whispered in her sister's ear when their father spoke up.

"We received a lot of information about the home from the realtor who sold us this place. The builder was a sailor and must have encountered a lot of albatross during his whaling adventures in the South Seas. You see the decorative white plaster relief of a sailing ship rising from the wall above the fireplace?" he asked when the constables peered into the sunroom. "We think it's a replica of his boat."

Alice and Emma were anxious to get to the matter of Murphy's bone, and hurried into the kitchen where it was resting in a clean cardboard box on the tiled counter. "The bone is in here," they called out together.

When their parents and the constables entered the room, Emma blurted, "We were eating dinner last night when Murphy came into the house and dropped it on the kitchen floor. It spoiled Mum and Dad's meal but we thought it was very interesting. Do you know what kind of a bone it is?"

The constables walked over to the box and

examined its contents. "I suspect it's a leg bone. A tibia probably. They're long like this one. But there's something a little unusual about it. We see a lot of bodies in our line of work, and the odd skeleton, but we don't always come across random bones that have separated from a skeleton. If we could match it up with skeletal remains, identification would be a lot easier," said Avery, who scribbled notes into a dog-eared notebook with the stub of a pencil.

"Quite often bones are carried off by wild animals or a dog that disturbs a burial site. That creates a problem," added Sullivan. "Our guys should be able to ID it. Don't worry."

"We certainly hope no more are found on our property," said the girls' father. "I questioned at first whether pranksters had tossed the bone over the hedge and Murphy picked it up. I also wondered if he dragged it home from somewhere. We have access to the back lane, but the gate is seldom open."

Their mother sighed. "It's frustrating not knowing where it came from. We hope it's not going to upset our lives. The girls will be starting school in a few weeks."

"We'll take it back to the lab and see what we can find out," Avery said. "Bone identification is the work of the specialists. When we have something, we'll be in touch, but just one more thing. When did you move in?"

"Two weeks ago," said Alice and Emma's dad. "We fell in love with the house and property as soon as we saw it. We were told that there have been two previous owners, the retired mariner and his wife, and the man we purchased the house from. His name is Rex Allen. He's a World War I vet and moved to a smaller place apparently. We've no idea how long he lived here. I'm sure the neighbours could tell you more. We haven't met them yet."

When Sullivan picked up the box and the officers got ready to go, Alice couldn't resist asking one more question. "Do you think it could be a dinosaur bone? You mentioned it looked unusual."

"You kids are keen listeners, and you really pay attention to detail. I'm impressed," said Avery. He and Sullivan headed for the door. "I don't think dinosaur bones would look like this one. But, if it turns out to be a dinosaur bone you'll be the first to know."

CHAPTER FOUR

After the constables left, the girls ran to the back yard to play on a swing which hung from a sturdy branch of the sprawling plum tree. The tree was old and had been planted many years ago a short distance from the lane which ran behind all the fenced and gated properties.

Most of the garden had been well looked after when the Eden family took possession of the home. But, the area behind the plum tree was a jumble of wayward blackberry bushes and morning glory vines which twisted and coiled around everything in their path. The twins' mother threatened to clear the whole mess away. Alice and Emma, on the other hand, liked the short-lived white flowers and thought they added colour to the laneway. They also enjoyed eating blackberries.

"Please Mum, leave the bushes alone," the twins said when their mother tackled weeds in the flower garden nearby. "We want to pick them when they're ripe and sell them at the front gate, along with the sour pie cherries and the Bing cherries, just like we did at the orchard in Summerland. We could sell raspberries and loganberries too if we have enough, and give fruit to the neighbours who don't have any. We can't eat everything ourselves. Remember how good we were at selling fruit last season?"

Mum smiled. "How could I forget? You had a ball. You're natural born salesgirls and sold more fruit at the roadside stand than all of us put together."

"So, what do you think? May we have a fruit stand?"

"That's a super idea. It would be a good way to meet the neighbours and perhaps some of the children you'll be going to school with. The brambles can be left alone for now. There's a lot of other work to do in the back yard. Let's see what happens. Now, go and enjoy the swing."

While Alice and Emma were swinging, they heard someone call out "Hi girls!" from next door.

Murphy barked as the twins looked beyond the raspberry patch to a back porch where a young woman was standing and waving. "Hello!" she said again. "I'm Nora. Welcome to the neighbourhood."

"Hi," the girls called. "We'll get our mother. She's wanted to meet the neighbours ever since we moved here." The girls ran off with Murphy, and returned with Mum who walked over to the fence to chat.

"I'm Emily Eden. Pleased to meet you."

"And, I'm Nora Stevenson. "It's wonderful to see a family move next door. Welcome."

"I'm Alice and this is Emma. We're twins," said Alice, something she always explained since her hair was light brown and straight as a poker while Emma's hair was red and curly as a corkscrew. "I'm taller than Emma, but we both have brown eyes. We don't look like twins. We're fraternal, not identical."

"That's nice," said Miss Stevenson. "It's a blessing to have a playmate in the family. I'm an only child."

"This is our dog, Murphy," said Emma. "He's usually pretty quiet, but he barks when he's excited. Like right now. He's wriggling all over.

He must like you."

Miss Stevenson bent down and patted Murphy who licked her hand. She laughed at his enthusiasm. "Dogs are very special. A long time ago when I was your age I used to play with a little girl who lived in your house. Her name was Heather. She also had a dog. I hope you girls will call me Nora," said the slender young woman with long black curls, dark brown eyes and dimpled cheeks.

Alice and Emma liked her instantly. "Is that okay, Mum? May we call her Nora?"

"If that's what she wishes, certainly," said their mother, tucking her wavy red hair behind her ears. "We're looking forward to learning more about the neighbourhood and the people who used to live here."

The girls were about to ask some questions when Mum said, "My husband, Jack, isn't home at the moment, but he'd like to meet you too. How about coming for tea? We can sit outside by the plum tree. It's a beautiful spot with the perennials in bloom."

"I'd like that very much," Nora answered. "Thank you."

"I've been meaning to get the wicker table and chairs set up, but with the thunderstorms lately I've delayed putting the furniture out. Now that the weather is nice your visit will be a good excuse to get it from the basement. I hope we can enjoy a few more weeks dining in the garden before fall arrives. Seeing as how it's Sunday tomorrow and Jack will be home, why don't you come over around two o'clock."

"That's perfect. I'm sure we all have great stories to share."

"Hooray," said the twins who hoped to make a new friend, even if she was almost as old as their parents. "We love company."

"Tomorrow it is then," said Mum. "Now I must finish the laundry. See you soon."

"Bye, Nora," said the girls.

Alice and Emma ran into the house and located the flowered chair cushions in one of the unpacked boxes downstairs, then dusted off the little brown wicker table and matching chairs stacked nearby. The next morning, when sunshine beamed through their closet window to herald a perfect day, the girls prepared for Nora's visit. After a quick breakfast, they carried the furniture out to the garden and set it beside the plum tree.

"You've picked the perfect spot, right beside the swing," said Mum. "It's a lovely place to visit. Let's hope our neighbour has lots to tell us."

"Her name is Nora," said Alice, always the one to remember everyone's name. Being the first born twin, she thought it was her responsibility to remember everything.

CHAPTER FIVE

Getting things ready for visitors was always a pleasure for Alice and Emma. They enjoyed fancy tea parties with their grandmother when she was alive, and appreciated her old English china and ornate cutlery. After helping their mother make scones, the twins wanted to choose the tableware.

"Is it okay to use Granny's china today?"

"If you're careful," said Mum.

The twins opened the door leading to the dining room filled with antique furniture and a china cabinet built into the wall. They unlatched the cabinet's leaded glass doors and took out their favourite tea cups and saucers featuring orange lilies, gold-trimmed rims and crown motifs stamped on the bottom. Just before Nora was expected to arrive, the girls took the china and cutlery outside and set it on the wicker table while Mum made the Nabob loose leaf tea. They returned to the kitchen to find Dad talking about the bone.

"Let's not bring up the bone business right now," he said. "Hopefully, Nora didn't see the police show up the other day. Keep your minds and ears open."

"Good plan," said Mum. "I've already told the girls not to mention it. They promised not to, and are pretty good at keeping secrets, aren't you girls?"

"Yes," said Alice and Emma, grinning at one another.

"That's great," said Dad. The story will be neighbourhood news soon enough."

When Nora arrived, she was carrying an armful of pink lilies and a little bag. The girls had seen her coming and rushed to the front door to welcome her. "Come in. Come in. Mum and Dad are in the kitchen. You're the first guest in our new home."

The girls were thrilled when Nora presented each of them with a box of Cracker Jacks. "We adore caramel popcorn! And we love collecting the charms inside the box. We have quite a collection now. We keep it in a secret place," Emma grinned, then looked sideways at Alice.

"How does the house look, Nora?" asked Alice when the girls gave her a tour of the main floor before making their way to the kitchen.

"I'm pleasantly surprised. "It hasn't changed much since I was here last. Except for most of the furniture, the place looks the same. Your parents have kept the albatross painting and the sailing ship relief I'm glad to see."

"We love all the neat things in this house," said Emma.

When they reached the kitchen, Nora handed the flowers to Emily who excitedly thanked her, then introduced her husband, Jack.

"It's great to meet you, Nora," he said with a smile and a handshake. "The house is grand. We love everything about it. You knew the sea captain and his family well, I understand."

"Yes. My mother and I knew the Stones for many years. We were great friends. Heather and I went to school together."

"It looks like a good place to settle down. We

enjoy the view of the mountains and the sea, though I must confess, compared to the sunny Okanagan at this time of year, it's been quite rainy." Everyone laughed, and then Alice spoke up.

"That was a scary thunderstorm the other night. Murphy leaped onto our bed and squished himself in between us underneath the blankets. The rain was pounding on the roof and the wind was whistling. The whale on the weathervane must have had quite a ride."

Emma chuckled at her sister's remarks. "I can laugh about it now, but I was really scared. Did the storm wake you, Nora?"

"It sure did. We do get a lot of rain here in winter, not so much in summer, but when we get a thunderstorm we often get downpours. The last storm was a monster."

Dad laughed. "It was a whopper, but rain's good for the garden. I can't get over how fast it has grown."

"Why don't you take Nora out to the garden now?" suggested Mum, "then we can have our tea."

The twins and Murphy led the way to the plum tree as Dad and Nora chatted away behind them. "Come and have a seat, Nora," said the girls, motioning toward the wicker furniture.

"Mum wants this to be a special place where she and Dad can relax and watch us play," said Alice, "so we put the furniture right beside the swing."

"It's nice here," said Nora. "It saddens me to think it's been more than twenty years since I enjoyed having lunch here with Heather and her parents."

"We're going to help Mum carry out the goodies now," said Emma. "We'll be back in a minute. Don't start your stories without us." The twins returned to the kitchen and brought out the scones, cream and sugar and their mother's raspberry jam and lemon curd on two separate trays. Mum followed with the china tea pot and set it on the table in front of Nora.

"Everything looks lovely. Are these your homemade goodies?"

"We helped make the scones. The raspberry jam and lemon curd are Mum's specialties," answered Emma.

Mum smiled. "Please, help yourself, while I pour you a cup of tea. Why don't you begin? Tell us about your life here and the sea captain who built this lovely place."

CHAPTER SIX

There's so much to tell," began Nora. "I never knew my father. I was born after he left to fight in World War I. Sadly, he was killed in action and never came home. My mother was very kind and went out of her way to make sure we had lots of fun together. She passed away just after I graduated from university. I stayed here, in the family home, and got a very interesting job." She smiled and leaned toward the girls. "I work at the museum where I identify old artifacts and bones."

Alice and Emma rolled their eyes and looked at one another with a playful grin when they heard the words 'museum' and 'bones.' "Ooh," they shivered, "that must be exciting."

"Very. Old bones have a story to tell," Nora winked before continuing her story. "My mother first met Rhys and Caroline Stone when they built your home in 1912."

Alice laughed. "We knew the house was old when we saw the brass number plaque over our front door. We think it looks nice."

"I like it too," said Nora. "It adds a bit of charm to the home. Anyway, Mr. Stone had spent many years at sea and was the captain of a whaling ship which sailed off the coast of South America. When he was in Colombia he became interested in emeralds and began importing them," Nora said, as she lovingly fingered a brilliant green emerald heart hanging from a gold chain around her neck. "This was a special gift from him when I was about your age."

"It's very pretty. I like the way it sparkles when the sun shines on it," said Emma. "We're really fond of jewelry and love looking at our grandmother's. She didn't have any emeralds though. Granny died before we moved back to North Vancouver."

"I'm sorry to hear that," Nora said sympathetically when she saw their sad faces. "Would you like to hear more?" The twins nodded their heads enthusiastically.

"Well, according to my mother, Mr. Stone was about fifty-five when he retired and settled down. His wife was thirty years younger. She was an English beauty, with porcelain-like skin, long chestnut brown hair and captivating blue eyes. Their daughter, Heather, was born in 1914, the same year I was. My first memories are of coming here to play with her on the swing," Nora laughed, pointing to the plum tree where the swing moved gently in the breeze. "It was made from rope Mr. Stone had knotted and a sturdy ship's plank, and here it is still."

"When we moved in, Dad put a new seat and rope on the swing," Alice said, enthusiastically.

"I'm happy to see you using it," Nora beamed. "Remember, I told you that Heather had a dog? When she was young, her parents got her a Great Dane puppy. Mr. Stone named him Neptune, after the mythical God of the Sea, and had a special collar made for him. You won't believe this, but it was studded with glistening green emeralds."

"Wow, an emerald collar? That's hard to imagine," said Emma while Alice and their parents looked on curiously.

"It was different and definitely striking,"

admitted Nora. "It looked good on Neptune. He was a magnificent dog, very affectionate, gentle, and good with children. He grew to an enormous size, nearly three feet tall at the shoulder, and weighed over 125 pounds. When he stood on his hind legs he was taller than Mr. Stone. He got lots of exercise romping in the garden with Heather every day. They were very close.

"Just before her twelfth birthday, Heather died suddenly from influenza. Her parents were devastated. I've never gotten over losing such a good friend. Just thinking of her brings tears to my eyes. Neptune missed her too. He sat sadly in the garden watching for her. Two years later he disappeared. No one knew what happened to him. Some neighbours thought he had been stolen."

"I'm sorry your friend died and that her dog disappeared," Emma said softly. "That's sad. We'd be heartbroken if something happened to Murphy."

"It was sadder still when a year later, Mr. Stone vanished during a violent late night thunderstorm. No one saw him again. I was fifteen then, and I can still remember that awful storm and the frightening flashes of lightning. Mrs. Stone seldom went anywhere after that. It was very strange.

"Some people believed the house became haunted. One day during a rainstorm when I ran to the corner store for a bottle of milk, I saw a shadowy figure looking through a telescope in the turret. The apparition was staring out to sea as if watching for a ship to come home. It really frightened me."

"Wow. You saw a real ghost? We've never seen one," said Alice. "We just knew there was a ghost living here." Alice looked at Emma whose eyes were almost popping out of her head. "What did your mother say?"

"Well, my mother wasn't pleased when I told her. She didn't want anybody suggesting that we had a ghost for a neighbour, and forbade me to talk about them again. I never spoke to anyone about ghosts until the day I mowed the grass for Nellie Johnson, an elderly widow who lived across the street."

"What happened?" asked Emma.

"While Mrs. Johnson worked in the back yard where she had a chicken house and several hens, I cut the front lawn. When I was finished I went to see her. There she was holding a chicken by the neck. She grabbed an axe, put the chicken's head over a chopping block and hacked its head off! Blood was spurting everywhere and the headless chicken took a couple of steps before it flopped motionless on the ground. I was horrified. I wanted to run, but I couldn't move."

"Ugh, that was awful," said Emma, while Alice screwed up her face in horror. "What happened next?"

"Well," Nora continued, "Mrs. Johnson asked me to wait while she went into the house to wash her hands, and get some money for me. When she came back she told me that she had seen a ghost in the turret during a thunderstorm. I told her I didn't want to talk about it, but she carried on about the driving rain, the howling wind and the brass weather vane that looked as though it was going to fly off the roof."

"Did you tell anyone about it?" Alice asked.

"No, and I never went back to cut the lawn again. But I was happy to learn that I wasn't the only one who had seen the ghost. She told me that no one believed her ghost story. I did, and I felt sorry for her, but the killing of the chicken affected me deeply. I've been a vegetarian ever since."

"Listening to your story is better than any

mystery book we've ever read," said Alice excitedly. "I can't believe all those awful things happened. It doesn't seem real."

"It was a long time ago. Times have changed and the neighbourhood has changed since I was a youngster. Many of the neighbours are new, the chicken houses have gone and so have the chickens. It's been lonely without a family next door. Mr. Allen, who used to own your house, didn't have any children. He never married. The elderly Scottish couple, Ann and Thomas McTavish who live next door to you, have been here forever. They're fond of children, but never had any either. I'm so pleased you've come to live here. Now, let's hear all about you."

"We love it here," said Emma. "Our bedroom is huge. It's the one with the hidden staircase that leads to the turret with its neat fire escape. There's a secret hiding place under the stairs, there's the telescope in the turret and we have a chicken house. That's so exciting."

"Yes. All those things thrilled me too when Heather and I used to play together. But, why is the chicken house exciting?"

"We want Dad to turn it into a little library for

us," answered Emma. "We've always wanted a place of our own where we could read our mystery books and write in our diaries. We could have shelves for our books and a table with chairs. We've still got some of Granny's old children's books from the 1800s. We loved the way she read the books to us in her dramatic English accent."

"And we've got some really old dictionaries too. We love old words. Dad built a wooden stand for the heaviest one which is full of some words people don't use anymore. Have you ever heard of a fizzog?" asked Alice.

"No, I have to admit I haven't," said Nora. "What is it?"

The twins giggled and threw their hands in the air when they yelled, "It's your face!"

Everyone laughed, including Dad who was listening intently to what the twins were saying. "The girls have been on about a little library from the moment they spied the chicken coop," Dad announced. "Are you trying to put pressure on me, girls?" he asked when they looked at him with a pleading smile. He tilted his head toward them, then looked at Nora.

"You can see what I'm up against. The girls

certainly have a lot of ideas and plans. Everything takes time. We've been busy ever since moving here so haven't had a chance to wander around the neighbourhood and meet anyone. I'm looking forward to reconnecting with old friends, making new contacts, and getting back into the real estate business as soon as I can."

Alice and Emma frowned, but Nora kept the conversation lively by asking the girls about their former home.

"Well, we grew up on a 10-acre orchard in Summerland on Okanagan Lake," said Emma. "Our granny lived in a house on the top of a hill nearby and we saw her every day. She taught us how to knit and play cards and we got to be real card sharks. She was so much fun, but then she got sick with gallstones and died. That's when our parents decided to sell the orchard and move back to North Vancouver where we were born."

Alice was anxious to change the subject to something that would interest Nora. "Have you ever heard of Ogopogo, Nora?"

"Yes, I have, but I don't know much about him. I know he's a legendary sea serpent and many people claim to have seen him in Okanagan Lake."

PENELOPE J. McDONALD

"We've seen him. We were swimming one day
at the beach and everybody got excited when a man
came running up the beach and said he had seen
Ogopogo off the point. Dad was taking photos of
the lake that day and we rushed over to see if he
could get a picture of him. We looked up and down
the lake but didn't see anything. Then, all of
sudden, there he was, swimming not far off shore.
He was very long and had fins on his back."

"He looked like a big eel with tiny ears on top
of his head," Emma added. "Everyone yelled and
pointed at him. Dad said he got a good picture of
him and developed the film in his darkroom.
Unfortunately, all he captured was a series of little
waves in a row, no Ogopogo. People have seen the
monster for years, going back to the late 1700s
when the local Indian tribe saw him. He's quite the
celebrity."

"That's true," said the twins' father. "And
Ogopogo *is* hard to photograph. He's there one
minute, gone the next. He sinks quietly below the
surface of the lake and doesn't leave much of a
wake. Many of our friends have seen him too.
Some people think he's a huge oarfish, but they
live in salty oceans, not freshwater areas. The local

newspaper often publishes pictures and first-hand stories of the creature, but of course the pictures are never very good, so I don't feel too badly." He laughed. "It was a very exciting day at the beach."

"We miss our friends in Summerland," Emma continued, "but we hope to make friends here when school starts. Right now we're making a fruit stand and when the fruit is ripe we'll sell some outside the front gate. We did that at the orchard. There's lots of different fruit here. We even have three kinds of cherries. When the peaches are ripe we'll be able to pick them from our bedroom window."

"I remember when some of those trees were so small they didn't produce fruit," said Nora, gazing wistfully at the mini orchard before her. "You should have a good crop to sell."

"The girls are always on the go," their mother said. "There's never a dull moment with twins. We hope this has been a good move for all of us, Murphy too."

"I'm sure it has," replied Nora. "I love it here and wouldn't want to live anywhere else. And now that you are here, I'll enjoy it even more."

Later, when Nora had gone home, Alice and Emma overheard their parents discussing the afternoon. "Nora is certainly frank, I can say that for her," said Dad. "That was a gruesome tale about the chicken getting axed. It must have had quite an effect on her. Did you see the look on the twins' faces? They were enthralled. I wouldn't be surprised if they become detectives when they grow up." He laughed. "Heaven knows they've read enough mystery books."

"Well, there undoubtedly have been a lot of weird things going on in this house," said Mum. "And we have a ghost living in the turret? The Stones had more than their share of tragedies in their life. Imagine losing your child to that dreadful flu, and then your dog and husband disappear. Poor Mrs. Stone. I can't imagine how she was able to carry on. I wonder what eventually happened to her."

"Mum and Dad are just as curious as we are," said Alice when she and Emma went upstairs to read. "I can't wait until tomorrow."

CHAPTER SEVEN

As soon as the portable fruit stand was finished, the twins began picking cherries from the lower branches of the tree while their mother and father gathered cherries higher up. Having fallen from a ladder in the orchard, and in her words 'I nearly killed myself,' Alice had no desire to step on a ladder again.

Selling cherries was not only profitable, but exciting for Alice and Emma. Before they knew it they had met some neighbours, including Mr. and Mrs. McTavish from next door. "Hi there lassies," said Mr. McTavish loudly in his thick Scottish brogue as he removed a plaid tam from his bald head. "So you're the ones who have moved next door. It's nice having young people around again. Have you seen the ghost yet?"

"Come on now, Thomas," said his wife, "don't

bother the girls with such talk. They're here to sell cherries today. Welcome to the neighbourhood," she said, her short silver curls shining in the sun and blue eyes twinkling. "What are your names?"

"I'm Alice and this is my twin sister, Emma. We're fraternal twins. I'm the oldest. I was born first," Alice said proudly.

"Oh," Mrs. McTavish said. "I bet you girls have a lot of fun together. We've seen you and your cute little dog playing in the yard. You must have been very busy lately picking these luscious Bing cherries. We'd like to buy a few, a pound maybe, please."

Emma selected the one pound weight and put it on the old brass balance scale before putting the cherries in the measuring scoop. When the scale balanced, she added a few more, then emptied the contents into a paper bag and handed it to Mrs. McTavish.

"No charge," said Emma with a smile. "We were going to bring you some cherries later this afternoon."

"We hope you enjoy them," said Alice.

"That's very kind of you. Thank you. Heather used to bring us fruit a long time ago," said Mrs.

McTavish pensively. "She was about your age then. We're very happy to see you here," she said, before linking arms with her husband and toddling home.

"She reminds me of Granny with her pretty silver hair," said Emma. "She's very nice. We're lucky to have good neighbours on both sides of us."

A bit later, the twins met two girls from down the block who were roller skating past the fruit stand and stopped to chat. They were sisters, Marie and Elizabeth, Lizzy for short. Both had blonde hair and dark blue eyes, and looked very much like sisters.

"We're going to North Star School and will be in grades five and six this September," said Marie, the eldest.

"We'll both be in grade six," Alice replied. "We've just moved into the house behind the hedge."

"You're both going to be in the same class?" asked Marie with a concerned look on her face. "Did one of you fail a grade?"

"No. We're twins," said Alice. "I know we don't look like it, but we are. I'm taller and we have different coloured hair. Emma has to fuss with her squiggly curls, especially when she wakes up in the morning, but my straight hair isn't any work at all. We aren't identical twins, we're fraternal twins. Are there many kids living around here?" she asked, not wanting to talk about being a twin anymore.

"A few. There are a lot more kids living on the next street down. You'll meet them all when school starts. Maybe we can go roller skating together some time," Lizzy said while Marie looked like she was still trying to believe the fact that the twins were really twins.

"We'd love to come skating sometime, maybe when we're not so busy. That would be fun," said Emma.

"Our Great-Uncle Rex used to own this house. We visited him all the time and played under the stairs and looked through the telescope. It was always fun, but now he's moved into a little house which isn't any fun at all," said Marie sadly.

"Why don't you come for a visit sometime?" asked Emma. "We found the little door that leads to the hiding place under the stairs. There's a lot of old stuff under there."

Lizzy laughed. "We know. There's a ghost in the turret too. Our great-uncle used to see him all the time. Have you seen the ghost? He likes to watch the thunderstorms."

Alice handed the sisters some cherries. "No, not yet," she answered. "Our neighbour, Nora told us about the ghost. And so did Mr. McTavish when we saw him today. We haven't spent much time in the turret yet. It's a really neat place."

"We'll talk to Mum and Dad about you coming over soon," said Emma.

As the girls skated off, more people came by for cherries and by mid-afternoon all the fruit had been sold. Alice and Emma packed up the stall and went in to tell their mother the good news.

CHAPTER EIGHT

W hen their father arrived home after a meeting the next day, the girls rushed to open the lane gate for the car so he could pull into the driveway.

Emma glanced at Alice, and whispered, "Let's remind him about a library now, before he goes in the house."

"Well girls, you're looking happy," said Dad when he climbed out of the car. "Have you made some friends?"

"We met two sisters yesterday and they want us to go roller skating with them. Their great-uncle used to own this house and they miss visiting him here. Maybe we can have them over sometime," Alice suggested.

"That's a super idea," said Dad, handing Emma his briefcase. "It will make the first day of school a lot more fun when you know someone."

Emma smiled, eager to make small talk before they asked about the construction project. "Did you have a good day, Dad?"

"I had a few meetings. Getting my real estate licence back again is going to take a while. After running an orchard for eight years, I'm a bit rusty. What are you girls up to?"

The girls exchanged glances and Emma gave Alice a nudge. "You go first," she whispered.

Alice crossed her fingers and spoke up. "Dad, we've been hoping that you can find time to begin the library project, like I mentioned when we were talking to Nora the other day. We've sold tons of fruit and put quite a bit of money in our bank account. We promise to help. Please, please, can we start it now?"

"Ask your mother what she thinks. We can talk it over during dinner. I'll be in the office full time soon, so maybe this would be a good time to start the project."

The girls ran into the house and helped Mum get dinner ready. When the family sat down to eat, Alice and Emma squirmed in their seats when they brought up the subject of the library. "Dad's okay with it Mum, what about you?" blurted Alice. "We could clean and paint, and help Dad rip out the dirty wooden floor. Nora will help too."

Mum chuckled. "You did a wonderful job with your fruit stand, girls. You've met some neighbours, and made friends. It would be nice to have a little library instead of a smelly old chicken coop in the back yard, wouldn't it? Sounds good to me."

"Boy, that was easier than I thought," said Emma when the girls got ready for bed.

"I can't believe it," said Alice. "I can hardly wait to get all the supplies and start work."

The next day, the family went to Paine Hardware and soon had everything they needed. As they went to leave the store, the girls spotted a wallpaper display on the opposite side of the room. When they rushed over to have a look, a nautical pattern caught their eye.

"Look at this wallpaper, Mum." Alice pointed enthusiastically at the display. "Blue and red sailing ships with white sails on the ocean."

"It would look fantastic in our room," said Emma. "Do you think...?"

"One thing at a time, you two. Let's get the library finished first. The wallpaper can wait. End of discussion."

"Can you believe that neat wallpaper?" Alice nudged Emma as they left the store. "There it was right before our eyes. It was meant for our room. We've got to get rid of that creepy ivy wallpaper before another thunderstorm comes and the scary faces stare at us again."

"The sailing ships are perfect," Emma agreed. "Let's hope that wallpaper will still be for sale when Mum and Dad decide to re-do the room."

Later, the girls saw Nora in the back yard and told her the good news. "We're starting work on the library tomorrow. Dad has the day off, and we've bought all the stuff we need."

"We're going to paint it white with green trim like our house," said Emma. "Why don't you come over in the morning to see what we're doing?"

CHAPTER NINE

Renovation of the chicken house was a cooperative effort with everyone, including Murphy, pitching in to help. When Nora popped over, the twins were overjoyed and full of questions as they scrubbed the outside of the little building together.

"What was it like when the chickens lived here?" Emma asked.

Nora looked wistful as she recalled the days when the chicken house was full of life and she and Heather fed the small bantam hens and gathered their little brown eggs.

"No chickens were killed at Heather's house," she told the twins. "You can't have eggs and eat your chickens too. Besides, they were far too cute to eat. When we were little, we had a lot of fun with those hens. Sometimes we dressed up Rosie,

Heather's favourite little hen, in a lacy doll's bonnet, then covered her with a blanket and put her in a doll buggy for a stroll around the garden. She was amazingly tame, and produced eggs nearly every day."

"What did Neptune think of the hens?" asked Alice.

"Neptune was a gentle giant," said Nora. "He loved everyone, even the hens. He didn't have a mean bone in his body. It was hard to believe that such a big dog could be so unruffled with the chickens running all around the back yard. They scratched at the ground and in the grass for bugs when they weren't cooped up in the chicken house. It was pretty noisy sometimes. He never stepped on any of them, or chased them."

"I don't know if Murphy would have been like that. He's so energetic and playful when he's with us. Look at him now." Alice laughed. "All he wants to do is have a water fight with the hose. You should have seen him when we first got out the soap and the scrub brushes and filled the pails with water."

In between water fights, scrubbing and washing and a break for lemonade, the twins and

Nora managed to get the exterior of the building clean enough for painting.

Dad walked over to the twins. "Let's tear up the floorboards now. The outside walls will need two days of hot sun to make sure the wood is dry enough for painting. I'll get a hammer and crowbar and get started."

"It will be good to get rid of those smelly boards, once and for all," Emma said firmly. "They really stink in this hot weather. We can help you, Dad. When you pull out the nails we'll put them in a pail so no one will step on them. Remember that time when Mum stepped on the rusty nail in that abandoned cabin in the woods when we went exploring? She had to have a shot so she wouldn't get lockjaw. We hate shots!"

"I do remember. Your mother's foot was sore for a long time."

Dad put the crowbar under the first board and pulled out a few nails, then moved to the next board. The screeching sound made by the nails as they were released from the old wood sent shivers down the twins' spines, like fingernails scraping down a blackboard.

Emma gritted her teeth. "They make such an

awful noise when you pry them up, like they don't want to be disturbed."

"They do make a funny noise, I agree. It's almost like a shriek for help." Dad chuckled and made a funny face.

After a few boards were gone, Dad caught a glimpse of something strange in the dim light beneath the floor.

"What's this?" he asked out loud, peering into the narrow space. He placed the crowbar under an adjacent board and pulled it back for a better look. "Oh, no!" he yelled, before tumbling backwards onto the pile which had already been removed. Nora and the girls scrambled to see what had frightened him.

"A skeleton! It's a skeleton," the twins cried in disbelief. "The bony arm of a skeleton."

Nora let out a blood curdling scream, and clasped her face with her hands when she saw that the skeleton was missing a little finger.

"Ooh! It's Mr. Stone," she shrieked, then fainted.

CHAPTER TEN

Y ou found a skeleton? Where?" Avery asked when he answered a call from Jack Eden. "Under the chicken coop? Good heavens. That must have been quite a shock." He waved excitedly at Sullivan who rushed over when he realized his partner was onto something big. Avery put his hand over the receiver as he listened to Eden's anxious tale and whispered in Sullivan's ear at the same time. "It's Jack Eden. He's found a skeleton."

"Okay, Mr. Eden. Take it easy. Don't pull up any more boards. Just leave the site as is. We'll be there shortly, and have our investigators begin an examination of the area immediately. The girls' library will have to wait." Avery hung up the phone and shook his head. "That's the end of our day in the office."

"So, what happened?" asked Sullivan.

"He found a skeleton with a missing pinkie on its right hand, of all things."

"Wow. That must have been frightening. I wonder what the twins thought. They must have been horrified."

"Never mind the twins. Nora Stevenson was there. She passed out when she realized who the skeleton was."

"Okay. Who was it?"

"The old sailor, Rhys Stone. She called out his name before she fell to the floor. Let's get over there. I'll alert the others and meet you at the car."

Though the twins were disappointed that the renovation was put on hold, they were intrigued at the prospect of an investigation and looked forward to watching the police do their work.

"It's unbelievable, and so sad," Emma told Alice. "Mr. Stone was like a Dad to her. I wonder what happened to him. All she could talk about was the missing little finger. I wonder what happened to it."

"Yeah," said Alice. "And I wonder what the skeleton looks like. We've never seen a real skeleton before. Do you think it's missing any more bones?"

"Good question," Emma said quietly. "When the neighbours see the police come and hear the skeleton being dug up, everyone is going to know something strange is going on at our house. Everyone already thinks we have a ghost in the turret. I wonder if this is a good time to tell Dad and Mum about the bone *we* found."

"They're upset enough," answered Alice, who always wanted everyone to be happy. "Let's wait to see what the skeleton looks like. If other bones are missing maybe we could get our bone from the closet to see if it's part of the skeleton. We don't know anything yet about the bone that Murphy found. I'm on pins and needles I'm so excited."

When the police showed up, Alice and Emma were waiting by the roadside.

"So, you've found a skeleton this time, girls," said Avery when he and Sullivan got out of their police cruiser and encountered the twins. The special investigators arrived in a separate vehicle and unloaded the boxes of equipment they needed.

The girls stood transfixed as the four-man team strode by with their gear and followed the constables through the gate into the property.

"Yes. It has a missing finger, and our neighbour Nora knows who it is," said Alice, excitedly. "It's in the back yard. We didn't see the whole thing. Just a bony hand and arm with a bit of rotted clothing. It was dark under the floor of the chicken house. Dad said we had to stop prying up the boards because it was a crime scene, so he called you right away. Now that you're here, we're anxious to see if the skeleton is missing any other bones."

"I hope your investigation won't take long," Emma complained. "We want to have our new library finished before school starts. Can we watch while you do your work?"

"If you promise not to get in the way." Avery warned.

"We can sit on the stairs leading to the garage." Emma pointed to the structure next to the chicken house. "The top step is pretty high so we can see everything from there, except for the inside of the chicken house. Can we see the skeleton when you dig it out? Will it be put in a big box?"

"We'll see. Your parents will be advised as to what's being done. Just sit on the steps and keep quiet so no one will know you're there." Avery raised his eyebrows and looked at the curious pair. "Have your parents ever said, 'Little children should be seen and not heard?'"

"Yes," said Alice. "We know exactly what that means. We learned a long time ago when to be low-key and silent. We're not little kids anymore, we're eleven years old, you know." They walked over to the stairs, sat down and watched the men enter the chicken coop.

Voices and prying sounds continued as the men worked to reveal a complete skeleton covered in cloth fragments beneath the old wooden floor of the coop. Flashbulbs, set off by a police photographer when he pressed the camera's shutter, shone through the chicken house window and helped record every detail surrounding the gruesome scene.

The twins' parents chatted briefly with the police from time to time as work progressed throughout the afternoon.

"Tell me more about your neighbour who said she recognized the remains," Avery asked the twins' father. "I'll have to get a statement from her."

"Nora, Miss Stevenson, is very upset. She went home to lie down for a while after her fainting spell. It was the shock of noticing the missing finger from the skeleton's right hand that caused her alarm. I don't know anything more than that."

While the twins watched the comings and goings from their vantage point, they heard the creak and groan of the old garage door behind them when it was opened from the lane. "Who is it?" yelled Emma. She jumped up and let out a shriek when no one answered, and almost fell from the steps. Avery, hearing the commotion, looked over and gave her a stern look. "Oops," she said, remembering that she had promised to be quiet. She frowned and shrugged her shoulders at the constable before turning around to see Nora, pale-faced and looking tired when she walked through the garage and joined them on the steps. "Thank goodness it's you. I didn't see you coming."

Nora was curious. "How's everything going? I saw you from my back porch after I got up from a rest and thought I'd come over and keep you company. I feel better now."

"We're being nosy parkers and keeping an eye on things. We can't help it. This is a very interesting mystery. We just got the evil eye from Constable Avery though." Alice pointed to the tall, dark-haired man who was looking their way and standing next to their father. "He seems to be the boss. He's the one who was asking Dad about you. He's quite nice, but feels that little children should be seen and not heard. I don't think he has any kids. We promised to be quiet. Then Emma let out a scream and spoiled everything."

"I couldn't help it. Nora frightened me. I was thinking about the skeleton being dug out of the dirt and its bony long fingers flopping onto the policemen's faces. Then the garage door squeaked like a scary movie," Emma said, sheepishly.

Nora shuddered, and then grinned at Emma. "Now, that *is* a chilling thought."

"Constable Sullivan, his partner, is a shorter man with dark blond hair," Alice continued. "He's in the chicken coop now with the investigators. He's easier going than Constable Avery. You can't miss him. He has pock mark scars on his face. Anyway, I overheard the police talking to Dad. He told them you were resting. Dad said he didn't know anything about the skeleton. Do you really think it is Mr. Stone?"

"I'm positive. His little finger was ripped off during an accident at sea many years ago. Whaling is a dangerous way to make a living."

"Ouch, that's awful," said Emma, frowning. "I bet that really hurt."

While Nora and the twins chatted quietly, Avery walked over to the trio. "Hi girls," he said, and then spoke to the striking young woman beside them. "The twins' father tells me you're Nora Stevenson."

"Yes. I'm Nora. Pleased to meet you."

"I'm Constable P.J. Avery," he smiled and shook her hand. "I imagine Alice and Emma have told you that I'm conducting an investigation into the discovery of the skeleton under the chicken house. I understand you know who it is. I'd like to take some notes if you don't mind."

"I don't mind answering questions at all," answered Nora, sadly, as the constable took his note book out of his jacket pocket and began to write. "I'm horrified at what's been found here. The skeleton is the remains of Rhys Stone, the retired sailor who owned this property a long time ago."

"Why do you say that?"

"He was a whaler for many years and lost the little finger on his right hand in a whaling accident. It was caught in a rope and torn completely from his hand."

"Is there anyone else in the neighbourhood who knew the man? Can anyone else verify your story? The missing finger could be a clue to the identity if nothing else is found. We're searching the area now for something significant like jewelry, a belt buckle or wallet. Pieces of clothing could also be a clue. In this case the body appears to have been here for a long time judging by the significant decay."

"Ooh, that's a morbid thought," Emma said quietly. "I bet we don't get to have a peek and find out for ourselves. It would be great to see what the whole thing looks like."

"Maybe we can sneak over and peek in the window," said Alice.

"And get ourselves into deep trouble?" Emma gave her sister a dirty look.

"To answer your question, constable, Ann and Thomas McTavish are the only people left in the neighbourhood who knew the Stone family. They live next door." Nora pointed to the elderly couple's home. "Mr. McTavish is hard of hearing, but they'd both be pleased to help with your investigation, I'm sure."

"Can you remember the last time you saw Mr. Stone?"

"That's a difficult question. I can't remember the exact date I saw him last, but it could have been the day before he disappeared during a thunder and lightning storm in July of 1929. I remember his wife, Caroline Stone, telling my mother that they had gone to bed and were awakened by loud thunder in the middle of the night. Mr. Stone was fascinated by lightning and went up to the turret to watch the storm, as he often did, and in the morning he was nowhere to be found."

"Was an attempt ever made to locate the man?"

"People searched for him, but no clues to his disappearance were ever found. It was very strange indeed for him to vanish like he did. Rumours abounded throughout the neighbourhood as to where Mr. Stone may have gone. He was originally from England and would have been about seventy-two then. At the time of his disappearance, he was healthy, in the prime of his life really, with a thick crop of curly white hair and beard. He was very handsome."

"What happened to Mrs. Stone? How old was she then?"

"Caroline was thirty years younger than Rhys and would have been forty-two. She stayed in the home for several more years, and eventually sold the property in 1940 to Rex Allen, the man the Edens bought the house from. I know it was 1940 because that's the year I got my Master's Degree in Anthropology."

"Rex Allen. Hmmm. The Edens mentioned his name when we were here a couple of weeks ago. Is the man still around?"

Nora was puzzled. "You've been here before?"

"Yes, just a minor matter. Have you any idea where Mr. Allen moved to?"

"No, I don't, but I'm sure he won't be hard to find. He's still living in the community." Nora turned, and looked thoughtfully at her new neighbours who were listening to the conversation nearby.

"Thank you, Miss Stevenson, you've been very helpful," Avery said before walking over to the chicken coop to see how things were progressing. He peeked through the doorway and signalled to his partner who had spent much of his time inside the coop taking notes while the investigators went over everything piece by piece.

"How's it going, Sullivan?" asked Avery when his partner stepped outside.

"I've never seen anything like it. Looks like the guy was wearing pyjamas when he died, but there's not much left of the fabric, or the flesh for that matter. The burned bits of cloth and the discoloured bones, especially around the chest area and back are particularly interesting. A lightning strike perhaps? No personal effects have been discovered yet. This is going to be a tough job for our guys in the lab."

Avery went inside the coop to speak to the investigators and have a good look at the exhumed body himself. He had to agree with Sullivan. He'd never seen a corpse which had obviously been burned through to the bone in a pinpointed area. Lightning was definitely a possibility, but that didn't explain how he ended up under the chicken coop.

"We're ready to call it a day," said one of the

investigators. "We'll come back tomorrow and take a good look around the chicken house and see if more bones are buried in the area."

Avery walked back to the onlookers and announced that the skeleton had been exhumed and was being taken back to the lab for analysis. "The area has been secured and we're wrapping up proceedings for today. There's still a lot of work to do. We'll see you sometime after 8:00am tomorrow."

Alice's curiosity got the better of her and she couldn't help asking the question that bothered her. "Is the skeleton missing any more bones?" she asked bravely, when the men started to leave.

"No," answered Avery, shaking his head.

"Keep clear of the chicken house girls," warned Sullivan. "And be sure Murphy isn't left unattended. We all know how he likes to dig up bones, right?" He smiled at the twins and glanced at their parents, then left with the others.

Alice and Emma shared a furtive glance and began to tremble. "We've got to get our bone checked out," Alice whispered to her sister. "Right away. It's not Mr. Stone's!"

CHAPTER ELEVEN

Prior to going home, the officers returned to the police station and soon had Rex Allen's new address. Nora Stevenson was right. The man had moved only a few blocks away.

"Let's swing by the house and see if he's home," suggested Avery. "It'll save us checking him out tomorrow. We need to have a chat with the McTavish couple too and see what they have to say."

"We should check on the status of the bone that the dog dragged into the Eden's house PDQ. I'm curious to see what it is. It's obviously not part of our skeleton. Do you think more are out there somewhere?" asked Sullivan as they drove.

"I was wondering the very same thing," Avery mumbled. "It was a relief to see that the skeleton was complete except for the pinkie. We'll have to take a really good look around the place tomorrow."

When the pair reached Rex Allen's neat little bungalow, they saw a tall and balding grey-haired man cutting the lawn in the back yard. They walked over to the cedar hedge and got his attention before he turned off the mower.

"Rex Allen?" Mr. Allen nodded his head and walked over to the constables who showed their identification and introduced themselves. "We'd like to ask you some questions, if you don't mind," said Avery, trying to hide his alarm when he saw the man's disfigured face.

"What about?"

"The property you used to own on West Kings Road. Avery and Sullivan took out their notebooks again and began jotting things down.

Avery continued the questioning. "You purchased the property from Caroline Stone several years ago and recently sold it to the Eden family?"

"Yes?"

"We've just dug up a body at your previous residence, actually a skeleton. Do you know anything about that?"

"Oh," said Mr. Allen with an anguished look.

His shoulders slumped, he looked defeated; he knew the jig was up. He invited the officers into his home and offered them a seat in the living room, before sitting down heavily on a recliner by the window. "I shouldn't have done it."

"You shouldn't have done what?"

"Buried Rhys Stone. I did it for her. She was desperate. It's a long, sad story. I don't know where to start."

A look of bewilderment came across the constables' faces. This wasn't at all what they expected to hear. Was it for real? Was the man delusional?

"Just tell us what happened," encouraged Avery who did his best to keep his composure.

"Two years before I went to war in 1914," began Mr. Allen, "Rhys Stone returned from the southern seas and his whaling adventures a rich man. He imported emeralds. He was a client of my father who was a jeweler and owned a successful jewelry business in downtown Vancouver. Rhys eventually met my friend, Caroline, and after a whirlwind courtship they were married. They built that lovely home, and filled it with all sorts of beautiful things. Two years after they married they had a daughter, Heather, and eventually got a Great Dane. No expense was too much for Rhys' beautiful wife, or his dog for that matter."

"What do you mean by that?"

"One of the most unusual pieces my father ever designed, with the help of a saddler, was a magnificent, fine-grained leather dog collar for Rhys' dog, Neptune. It contained five large emeralds which were held in place by elaborate gold fittings."

"Hmmm, that *is* interesting." Avery raised his eyebrows and glanced over at Sullivan who was scribbling as fast as he was.

"Caroline was twenty-five when they wed," continued Mr. Allen, "quite a prize for a man thirty years her senior. I only wish I had asked her to marry me first." He sighed heavily, and looked pale. "I need some water. It's hot out there today."

"I'll get you a glass," said Sullivan who had noticed the little kitchen off the living room on the way in and was anxious to keep the man talking. In a cupboard near the sink he found a glass, and let the tap run for a while before filling the tumbler with water. He returned to the living room and handed it to Mr. Allen. "Drink this. It's cold," said the constable impatiently. Mr. Allen looked up, took the glass and drained it.

"Please continue," said Avery while he adjusted his position on the chesterfield and got ready to write again. Mr. Allen took a deep breath and began to speak slowly and softly as the constables looked on with professional reserve.

"Caroline came to Canada from England with her parents when she was young and moved into the home next to me where I lived with my parents. We were both six years old then, and began school together. She was a pretty little girl with long chestnut brown hair and unusual blue eyes, the colour of a tropical ocean. I was captivated from the moment I met her. She had a refined English accent and was poised and shy, so different from all the other girls I knew. We were friends for many years and always stayed in touch, even after she married. When I returned from World War I, I was despondent for a long time, thanks to a head injury, though I was pleased to see how happy Caroline was, especially with little Heather. Caroline didn't let many people into her life, but she trusted me and valued my friendship, and I was thankful that Rhys was so good to her. I was thrilled when they asked me to be Heather's godfather. I never married. One could say that I lived my life vicariously through them; they were such a happy family, before the tragedies. Who would have believed that a flash of lightning destroyed everything that was left?"

"Tragedies? A flash of lightning? What's all that about?" asked Avery as he turned the page of his notebook and looked Mr. Allen directly in the eyes.

"It's hard to talk about the catastrophes still, even though they began in 1926 when Heather was just twelve. She died of the flu. Two years later, Neptune, their beautiful Great Dane, went missing. They were heartbroken, but carried on despite everything. They loved one another very much. As fate would have it, Rhys died unexpectedly, in 1929, when he was struck by lightning in the turret atop their home. Caroline asked me to bury him. I shouldn't have, but I did. It's hard to believe that was twenty-one years ago."

"You buried him? Where? Why?"

"Underneath the floor of the chicken coop," answered Mr. Allen, sadly. "It seemed the perfect place—under cover, away from the elements like

Caroline wanted. The chickens were long gone then."

Avery and Sullivan locked eyes and didn't move a muscle. Then Avery said, "How did you know it was the lightning that killed him?"

"You could see where the lightning had struck him, in the chest near his heart I presume. His clothes were burned. He was dead when I got there."

"You didn't call a doctor, or the police for help? Did you ever report the incident?"

"No. Caroline persuaded me not to. She was in a terrible state, and had been for a long time. The loss of her daughter haunted her. Rhys had always been there to comfort her, and now he was dead. She didn't know what to do other than call me for help. She was mentally unstable and worried constantly about being put in a mental institution. I was the only one she could depend upon. I couldn't let her down. So, in the middle of the night, I buried Rhys. I knew it was wrong, and I'm sorry I did it."

Avery and Sullivan were speechless. Never before had they heard such a sombre story and remorseful confession. This was definitely a case for the record books.

Avery took a deep breath and stood up to leave. "Thank you for taking the time to explain all this. We've unearthed the skeleton from the chicken coop. There is a lot of investigative work to do before anything can be determined as to how the case will be handled. You realize that if your claim is true, you broke the law when you interfered with a body instead of calling the authorities."

"Yes, I understand that."

"We appreciate your cooperation. Don't leave town. We'll be in touch again soon, Mr. Allen."

"I'm not going anywhere."

CHAPTER TWELVE

The constables returned to their car and headed back to the police station. "What do you think happened to Mr. Allen's head?" Avery asked Sullivan. "That's an awfully deep hole in his forehead. Must be the war injury he was talking about. Shrapnel maybe. It's impacting his eye. Did you notice how he squints?"

"Yeah. Nasty wound," answered Sullivan. "It's as big as a golf ball, poor guy. I wonder if it affects his ability to think properly. That was quite the confession, eh? We've got to locate Mrs. Stone and get her side of the story."

When they reached the police station, the office was already abuzz with the news that a skeleton had been taken to the morgue.

"Have we got an odd case for you," said Avery, when he and Sullivan found Detective Luigi

Lombardi in the lunch room. "You're going to love this one."

The constables told the detective all that happened that day, and noted how tired he looked. His black hair was streaked with grey, his skin was pale and his sad-looking brown eyes were sunk deeply in their sockets. Avery understood heavy caseloads and noted that the dark bags under his superior's eyes were getting worse.

"I heard you two were working on something different," said Lombardi. "The skeleton is being examined as we speak. When you and Sullivan have your notes in order, let me know. I'll swing by the place tomorrow and take a look at what's going on. I'm just finishing a coffee, then I'm out the door."

"Avery and I will be back at the crime scene tomorrow morning. We've got another interview scheduled with some neighbours. We'll see you there," said Sullivan.

CHAPTER THIRTEEN

Now that the chicken coop renovation was on hold, the twins were looking for something to do. They had already taken Murphy down the back lane and around the block for a walk. The constables were back on the scene, and a couple of investigators were continuing their search in the back yard so Murphy still wasn't free to run as he pleased.

"Let's ask Lizzy and Marie over," suggested Emma. The girls walked over to the raspberry patch where their mother was picking berries for dinner. "Murphy's had his walk and now we're bored. May we have Lizzy and Marie over for a while?" asked Emma.

"We'd rather have fun than watch the policemen today," Alice said. "We'll keep out of the way and won't go in the back yard. We want to check out things in the house anyway."

"Sounds like a good idea," said Mum.

The twins laced up their roller skates and raced down to Marie and Lizzy's home where the sisters were cooling off under the sprinkler on their front lawn.

"Come and join us," said Lizzy.

"We haven't got our swimsuits on," said Emma. "Why don't you both come up to our house so we can do some exploring."

"You've probably been up the turret tons of times with your great-uncle and know all the interesting places to visit. Maybe you can show us a few with the telescope. The only place we recognize is the Lions Gate Bridge," said Alice.

"That would be fun. We really miss our visits to great-uncle's house. We'll change and get our skates on, and let our mother know where we're going. Be right back," said Lizzy.

When they arrived at Alice and Emma's, the foursome went in the basement door and snuck under the stairs to check out the odds and ends left behind by Lizzy and Marie's great-uncle when he moved out.

"I guess great-uncle couldn't fit everything into

his new house," said Lizzy as shafts of sunlight fell through the cracks in the stairs and partially lit the dim area laden with relics from the past.

"Maybe he didn't want the stuff. Some of it is pretty old. There are jars of nails and screws here, a whole bunch of tools, his old fishing rod and tackle box." Marie lifted the objects, one by one, for a closer look. "Be careful, there are always lots of spiders and cobwebs here. Ooh," she shouted in disgust, when a large cobweb brushed against her arm and clung to her sleeve. "It can be creepy under the stairs. We need more light."

Lizzy, knowing where the light switch was, turned it on. With the area brightened a bit more, objects in the farthest corners became more recognizable.

"Hey, look at this," Marie called out. "Here's great-uncle's old army helmet. He brought it back from the Great War. He never wanted to part with it. It saved his life." She frowned, and lifted it from the nail it hung on. "What's it doing here? Why didn't he take it with him?"

"Maybe you should take it and give it back to him," suggested Emma. "He'd probably like to have it."

"Yeah, that's a good idea," said Lizzy. "You can come with us if you want."

After deciding that there wasn't much of importance left to look at under the stairs, the girls took the battered helmet with them, and headed to the turret for a lesson in geography.

"That's downtown North Vancouver, of course," said Lizzy as the twins took turns peering southward through the telescope. "Look at the waterfront. Do you see the ferry docked at the foot of Lonsdale? You can travel from there across Burrard Inlet to Vancouver. Sometimes great-uncle takes us over town to the Army & Navy store. They sell all sorts of stuff. We go on the ferry with our parents too, usually to shop at Woodward's Department Store for $1.49 day specials. Behind us you will see Grouse Mountain where people ride the chairlift to ski in winter."

"Is that Stanley Park where all the trees are?" asked Emma when she turned the telescope westward to look at the Lions Gate Bridge.

"Yes," answered Lizzy. "There is a zoo there with bears, monkeys, penguins and other animals, and visitors can rent a rowboat on a little lake called Lost Lagoon. You can walk along trails through the forest where huge cedar trees are over a hundred years old. There's even a hollow one so big that a car fits inside it."

"Really? Is that true?" asked Alice.

"It is," said Marie. "Dad parked our car in the famous hollow tree and we all stood beside it and had our picture taken. It's amazing to see trees that grow so huge. When we have out of town visitors we take them for picnics in the park."

While Alice was listening to the conversations, she was also gazing around the room and seeing all sorts of fascinating things. "A picnic in the park sounds good," she said absent-mindedly, running her fingers over some items on a desk.

"All the things in the turret used to belong to the sea captain," said Marie when she noticed Alice's interest. "Here's a compass and this is a sex...something," she began, then frowned when she realized she'd forgotten the word for the marine instrument. The others snickered and cupped their hands over their mouths when they heard the word sex.

"I think it's a sextant," said Lizzy, in an effort to ease Marie's embarrassment. "I'm sure that's what Great-Uncle Rex called it."

"That's it, I remember now," said Marie laughing at herself before continuing her commentary. "You see that old brass bell on the wall there? It's hanging from a white cord which was probably hand-knotted by Mr. Stone. There's another one attached to the clapper. Sailors used to do knotted work to pass the time when they spent long weeks at sea. It's called macramé."

The girls walked over to the bell for a closer look at the handiwork. Emma, anxious to hear what the bell sounded like, grabbed the clapper cord and swung it hard from side to side. Everyone covered their ears when the sharp ring echoed through the turret.

"Wow. That would sure get everyone's attention on the ship." Emma laughed and shook her head.

"You'll find some old papers in the drawers and on the shelves here—maps and things like that. Great-Uncle Rex wasn't fond of sailing or going out on the ocean much, but he did like to fish the Capilano River. He left all these things behind for the new owners," Lizzy said. "Perhaps your father would be interested in this stuff."

"Maybe," said Alice, thinking that she'd like to

come back to the turret with Emma later and take a closer look at everything before their parents did. She felt that something of interest was waiting to be discovered.

Before they left the turret, the twins swung the telescope northward for a closer look at the mountains. Just then, they heard the unmistakable sound of digging in the back yard. They hadn't mentioned finding the skeleton in the chicken house, nor had Lizzy and Marie noticed the unusual goings-on, until now.

"What's that noise?" asked Marie.

"It's just someone digging in the garden," answered Emma when she saw one of the investigators beside the chicken house.

Lizzy and Marie looked toward the sound and saw a man digging a wide hole. "What's he digging for?"

"We don't know," answered Alice. "But, we might as well tell you that a skeleton was found in the chicken coop, so there's a big investigation going on now to find out who it is. The bones have been buried a long time. It has nothing to do with us, that's all we know."

"A skeleton? Wow," said Marie. "A lot of

people have seen a ghost in the turret. That's the rumour going around. But, a skeleton in the chicken house? That's so neat."

"Well, it's not neat as far as our parents are concerned," said Emma. "They're very upset. But, to tell you the truth, we think it's exciting too. We saw one hand of the skeleton and its little finger was missing. That was really scary. Talking to the police about it and watching the investigators work was a lot of fun yesterday. We promised not to bother them today."

"I'm sure the whole neighbourhood is going to know about the skeleton soon. When we know whose it is, we'll let you know," added Alice.

The twins led Lizzy and Marie down the narrow staircase to look for their mother.

"There you are," Mum said when the girls found her in the kitchen. "Did you have a good time in the turret? I heard you up there."

"We saw some things through the telescope that we didn't know about. We'll tell you all about it later. We should take Murphy for another walk now. He's been cooped up far too long. We'll probably go to the corner store and get some jawbreakers and Double Bubble gum with our pocket money. Do you need anything?" asked Alice.

"Some whipping cream would be nice. You know how your father loves it with raspberries." Mum handed the twins some money, and with coins jingling in their pedal pusher pockets, they left.

"We can go and see Great-Uncle Rex tomorrow so we can take his helmet to him if you want," said Lizzy. "We'll ask our mother if we can go, then see if he'll be home. He loves to see us, and he'd like to meet you. He doesn't have any children of his own, so we are sort of like the grandkids he never had. A lot of people think he is our grandpa."

Emma was anxious to go. "I'm sure it will be alright. Is his house near here?"

"We can walk there," said Marie.

CHAPTER FOURTEEN

When Avery and Sullivan arrived at the Eden residence the next day, the twins were nowhere to be seen. "Where are the girls?" asked Avery. "They're usually here to greet us."

"You just missed them," said their mother. "They've gone to visit Rex Allen. Apparently, he's the great-uncle of their friends who live down the street. It's a small world, isn't it?"

Avery lifted his eyebrows in surprise. "Are those little sleuths up to something we don't know about?"

Their mother laughed. "No. I don't think so, but you never know with the twins. They've always got something up their sleeves. They were playing under the front stairs yesterday with Lizzy and Marie and came across Mr. Allen's old army helmet collecting dust in a corner, so they've gone to return it to him, that's all. I don't think they'll be long."

"Okay," said Avery, "thanks. We'll take a quick look in the back yard and see how the investigation is progressing before going back to the office. We'll be back later to interview the McTavishes. The girls should be home by then."

"What do you think we should do?" Sullivan asked as he and Avery left. "Do you think the twins are okay with Rex Allen? I'm still thinking about his bizarre confession. Should we drop by his house and check on them?"

"I think they'll be fine. He's Lizzy's and Marie's great-uncle. Why don't we go back to the office and find out when Lombardi's free so we can set up a time to interview Mr. Allen? Then we can casually drop by to let him know. That way we can see if everything is okay."

"Let's do that," said Sullivan. "I've become pretty fond of the twins."

Avery smiled. "So have I."

CHAPTER FIFTEEN

How much farther is it?" asked Alice, who was enjoying the walk in a new neighbourhood.

"There's Great-Uncle Rex's house." Marie pointed up the street to the little blue and white bungalow with the cedar hedge.

"Don't be afraid when you see him," warned Lizzy. "He has an awful dent in his forehead and he looks scary. That's why his army helmet has a big hole in it. We're used to the way he looks and hardly even notice it. He's really nice."

When the girls reached Mr. Allen's home, they were startled to see a dishevelled grey-haired figure in a long black coat rushing full speed out the back door. They screamed in horror when the person sprinted across the lawn, opened the back gate, and took off down the lane.

"Holy cow! Who the heck was that? It's not your great-uncle playing tricks on us, is it?" asked Alice, thinking about the disfigured face she was about to encounter.

Lizzy's eyes were just about popping out of her head. "That was really scary. I don't know who that was."

"Me neither," said Marie, "but whoever it was, they're very creepy. Great-Uncle Rex is a lot taller than that. He wouldn't be playing tricks on us when he's expecting us to visit. He wouldn't be wearing a silly long coat in this hot weather either. He doesn't even have a coat like that. It looked like a witch to me."

"Whoever it was, it frightened me too. Does your great-uncle have a friend who's a witch?" asked Emma as the girls climbed the front steps. Suddenly, they heard the front door being unlocked. When Mr. Allen opened it, he looked as though nothing had happened.

"Hi Lizzy and Marie. "I'm happy you've come to visit and brought your friends."

"Who just ran out your back door?" asked Marie. "We were all frightened half to death."

"It was just a friend who came to see me. She

doesn't like strangers," admitted Mr. Allen. "Sometimes she dresses differently, that's all. She took off running when she saw you walking up the street and I told her you were coming to see me. Don't worry about it."

Alice and Emma were dumbfounded by Mr. Allen's comments. For a moment they felt like their feet were glued to the doorstep. They didn't want to go inside the house. Alice, who just wanted to get rid of the helmet, regained her confidence and said, "I'm Alice and this is my twin sister, Emma," trying hard not to stare at the squinting eye and frightening hole in the old soldier's forehead. "We're the ones who are living in your old house. You forgot your army helmet under the stairs, and we thought you'd like to have it back." She stepped forward and placed it in Mr. Allen's arthritic hands.

"That's very nice of you girls, thank you," said Mr. Allen. "It was such a long time ago when I was wounded." He rubbed his head pensively. "The headaches still bother me at times. I'm not complaining, mind you. I lost a lot of my friends in that dreadful war. Come in. I'll show you an old picture."

Lizzy and Marie stepped inside first, and then

Alice and Emma followed. Mr. Allen walked over to the fireplace and placed the helmet on the mantlepiece beside a sepia-coloured photograph of himself and some of his buddies in uniform.

"Have you seen a photograph like this before? They're a tan colour because of a chemical process that was used to print photographs before black and white pictures evolved and became popular. The helmet and the photograph look good together, don't they? It's nice to have it back.

"But tell me, Alice and Emma, have you seen the ghost in the turret yet? I saw it several times when I lived in the old house. It haunted me, but since I've been here, I've not seen it again."

"We haven't seen the ghost," said Emma, "but we see eerie faces behind the leaves of the wallpaper in our bedroom when there's a thunder and lightning storm. They're really spooky."

"Sometimes we have a feeling that someone is watching us," added Alice, "but we're not afraid. It's the ghouls that really frighten us."

Mr. Allen's good eye squinted and he had a faraway look in his eyes. "Ghosts are strange things. Next time there's a storm brewing and the weathervane is buffeted by the wind, run outside and cast your eyes toward the turret. You may see him. The ghost loves storms."

Alice and Emma were uneasy. "We should go," said Alice. "We told our mother we wouldn't be long. We just wanted to return your helmet."

"We'll come by another day," said Lizzy.

Alice and Emma hurried outside with the sisters while Mr. Allen stood in the doorway and waved goodbye with a lost look on his scarred face.

CHAPTER SIXTEEN

T he constables dropped by after you left," said their mother when the girls returned home.

Alice chuckled. "We saw them driving by when we were walking back and they waved to us, but all of a sudden they turned their car around and drove toward the police station. We wanted to talk to them about our visit to Mr. Allen's place."

"They'll be back this afternoon to interview the McTavishes, so you can speak to them then. Did you see anything interesting at the old soldier's house? I bet he was happy to get his helmet back."

"He was. He put it on the mantlepiece beside an old army picture," said Emma, "but we didn't want to stay long." The twins purposely avoided their mother's question about seeing anything interesting. They wanted to speak to the police about the witch first.

After lunch the girls played table tennis in the front yard where their father had set up saw horses for the special green table with its little net. Both were good players, and the competition was intense.

"I'm tired of playing this," said Emma after a few powerful volleys from Alice. "You're smacking the ball too hard and I can't hit it anymore. Let's have a game of jacks on the sidewalk while we wait for the constables." Before Emma could grab the jacks from their bedroom, the police car arrived.

Emma snickered. "I can hardly wait until we see the expressions on their faces when we tell them about the witch."

"Hi, girls. You're looking very cheerful. It was nice to see you out today for a walk. Did you enjoy your visit with your friends' great-uncle?" asked Avery.

"Sort of," replied Alice, "but we want to tell you about the spooky witch we saw."

"A witch? Where did you see a witch?" asked Avery, putting his hand over his mouth to smother a chuckle when he glanced at Sullivan who had raised his eyebrows in a quizzical look.

"We saw the witch at Mr. Allen's house. She ran out his back door in a big hurry just as we got there," Alice answered.

"What did she look like?" continued Avery, trying to sound serious.

"She was creepy looking and wore a long black coat. Her hair was dreadful. It was all tangled, like it had never been combed. It's a wonder she didn't wear a pointy hat."

"That's very interesting," commented Sullivan. "Did you ask Mr. Allen about her? Who she was, why she was there?"

"Yes, we did. He said she was a friend and we shouldn't worry about it, and that she didn't like strangers. We felt uncomfortable, so we didn't stay long after we gave him his old army helmet," Emma said.

"We were so scared that we didn't want to mention the skeleton in the chicken coop or Murphy's bone, and the police coming to our house either," blurted Alice. "I think you should stake out Mr. Allen's place, and find out who the witch is. Maybe she'll go back there again."

"We'll have a visit with Mr. Allen soon," said

Avery. "We'll ask him about his visitor, and think about a stakeout. Just make sure you tell your parents about the witch. In the meantime, we're off to interview the McTavishes."

CHAPTER SEVENTEEN

While Avery and Sullivan interviewed Mr. and Mrs. McTavish beneath an awning on their back porch where it was cool, Alice and Emma hung the laundry on their back yard clothesline just a stone's throw away. Not only did they have full view of the officers and the elderly couple, but they could hear every word.

"We've come to talk to you about the skeletal remains that were found in the old chicken house next door," began Avery. "Nora Stevenson believes the bones belong to Rhys Stone. We're gathering information from as many sources as we can in an effort to solve this baffling case. You've lived here a long time and were friends of the Stone family?"

"Yes. Like the Stevensons, we were already living here when Rhys and Caroline built their home. We've been anxious to talk to you. How can we help?" asked Mr. McTavish.

"Perhaps you could tell us a bit about the Stones, what their life was like. Did you know about Mr. Stone's emerald collection? Did they have any enemies?"

The girls' ears burned while they attached the damp clothes to the line with big wooden pegs and listened for Mr. McTavish's reply. "Let's take our time. We've got to hear all of this," Alice said quietly.

"We were well aware that Mr. Stone imported emeralds as a result of his whaling adventures off the coast of South America," said Mr. McTavish.

"When Rhys became engaged to Caroline he thrilled her with an unusually large, deep green emerald ring which was worth a pretty penny. After they married, he had emerald jewelry custom-made for her—bracelets, broaches, necklaces and earrings set in gold—which she wore at tea parties in their garden. She was dreadfully spoiled. When Rhys had an exotic emerald dog collar made for their Great Dane, it didn't sit well with Caroline. She was jealous and complained that it was an inappropriate use of valuable gems. Maybe it was, but she had more emeralds than she could count. It caused a tremendous strain in their otherwise happy relationship."

The girls exchanged glances and their eyes grew wider as they listened. "This is fun," said Emma. "It's so interesting hearing about all the glamorous jewelry. Granny would have loved it."

Alice nodded with a big smile, hoping that the constables didn't realize they were snooping.

Avery raised his eyebrows. "That's quite something," he remarked, "having all that jewelry made. The garden parties must have been quite the gala affairs."

"They were. Ann and I were always invited," said Mr. McTavish. "It was a shame he spoiled her like that. But, they both loved emeralds. Rhys had his own collection. To keep them safe, he stored different shapes, sizes and colours in little gem sacks which he hid around the house. Their location was kept secret from Caroline in order to preserve his investment. He was afraid she'd sell them all and there would be nothing left for their old age. She was a terrible spendthrift.

"The biggest emeralds, his favourites, were those in Neptune's collar. He never worried about the dog or his collar being stolen. The lane gate was safely secured and the huge dog was never out of his sight. Rhys simply enjoyed looking at the Great Dane and admiring the gems. It was an infatuation with him. The emeralds around Neptune's neck were to be Heather's one day, for her education, he told me. Her unexpected death at age twelve changed everything."

"Wow. Gem sacks full of emeralds were hidden in our house," said Alice.

Emma's eyes flashed with excitement. "I wonder if they're still there. We've got to see if we can find them."

"Please continue," said Avery.

"Neptune's sudden disappearance a couple of years later saddened everyone. Subsequently, when we learned that Rhys vanished during a thunder and lightning storm, we were stunned."

"All this is very enlightening, and it must be difficult for you to speak about it. But, do you remember anything about the night Mr. Stone went missing?"

"We were awakened by the storm but eventually went back to sleep," Mr. McTavish advised.

"Our bedroom is on the opposite side of the house. We can only see the turret from the dining room," said his wife. "We never got out of bed."

"Caroline tearfully advised us the next day that Rhys had been in the turret at the height of the storm, but in the morning he was missing. Despite an extensive search he was never found. Caroline claimed she had no idea where he would have gone. She was in a bad state. When Rhys' ghost started frequenting the turret and was often seen by the neighbours, she completely broke down. I saw the ghost too, usually when the wind spun the weathervane around and thunderclouds raced across the sky."

Mr. McTavish's eyes looked sad and his face was ashen. "For years she remained a recluse. Rex Allen had been a school chum of Caroline's and was a close friend of the family. He helped her cope as best he could, but she eventually decided to move, and sold her home to Rex. No one, not even Rex, knew where she went. I have no idea where she is today."

"This is *so* interesting," said Emma, leaning closer to Alice. "We've nearly hung all the wash. I hope they're finished soon." Alice could hardly keep still she was so excited. With her back to the fence, she looked at Emma and gave her the thumbs up.

"Before you go, I should mention that I first met Rex many years ago when Rhys re-wrote his will after Heather's death. Rex was appointed executor, and I witnessed the document. It wasn't until Rex purchased the Stone residence years later that we got to know him well.

"To know that Rhys was buried in his back yard all this time is heartbreaking. Someone must know what happened—why Rhys was buried and who buried him. He was a nice person, a good neighbour and trusted friend. He didn't have any enemies to my knowledge," lamented Mr. McTavish.

When their job was done, the girls turned a few cartwheels before playing tag with Murphy on the lawn. Just then, Avery and Sullivan got up and stretched their legs. Mr. and Mrs. McTavish rose from their chairs and led the constables down the hallway.

"You've provided us with helpful information regarding this unusual case. Thank you," said Avery. "We'll contact you again if need be."

"It's nice to see you help your mother with the laundry," Avery smiled when he and Sullivan walked next door to see the twins. "That's a big job when you have a family, especially one with girls who are always changing their clothes. I have a couple of sisters who were quick change artists when they were young."

The girls chuckled. "We don't mind hanging the laundry, in summer. In winter it's a chore, especially when it's really cold. Last winter, when we lived on the orchard, it was so cold that the clothes froze hard as a board and we had difficulty getting them off the line. Then we had to let the clothes thaw out and dry around the stove before we could put them away," laughed Emma.

Alice looked at Avery. "We change our clothes all the time. That's what girls do. We're going shopping for some new school outfits soon."

"That's a good idea. Do some shopping and sightseeing, and enjoy yourselves before you hit the books again. You deserve it after all you've been through since moving here," said Sullivan.

"This summer has been one to remember. Alice and I are having a ton of fun," Emma giggled. "How many kids get to see a real skeleton and have

PENELOPE J. McDONALD

a detective dog who finds bones?"

"And see a shimmering emerald heart like the one that Nora wears around her neck," added Alice. "She was wearing it the other day when she came for a visit. This place is very special."

"Have you told your parents about the witch yet?" asked Avery.

"We told Mum when she was washing the clothes in the wringer washing machine. She wasn't very happy about it, but was glad that Lizzy and Marie were with us. We said you know about it, and that made her feel better. We were afraid that if we told her she wouldn't let us go there again," said Alice.

"That's good. Don't keep any secrets from your parents, girls. Sometimes secrets come back to haunt you."

When the constables left, the girls started giggling. "I love being a spy, don't you, Emma? It was good to hear that Neptune had an emerald dog collar, just like Nora said. It must have looked like big green Christmas lights around his neck. Now, I'm even more excited about solving this mystery. Who buried Mr. Stone? And where are the emeralds? I just know that the witch has something to do with our mystery. I've got an idea. Why don't we stake out Mr. Allen's house ourselves? If we see her, we can follow her."

CHAPTER EIGHTEEN

Well, that was an informative afternoon," Avery commented as he and Sullivan headed toward the police station. "This case has a lot of twists and turns. I've never done so much note taking in my life. I'm getting writer's cramp."

Sullivan laughed. "The ongoing adventures of our little private eyes continue to amaze me. I wonder what the witch was all about."

"That reminds me," said Avery. "Mr. Allen's coming in for another interview tomorrow. Lombardi's chomping at the bit."

"How did you get Mr. Stone's body out of the turret?" Avery asked Mr. Allen, following up on the man's confession of interfering with a dead body when they had visited his home.

"Down the fire escape," answered Mr. Allen who gazed at Avery with gloomy looking eyes as he sat in Detective Lombardi's office at the police station. "It took both Caroline and I to get him to the ground, then over to the chicken coop. It was dark—the middle of the night. It was raining heavily, and I was trying hard not to drop the flashlight I carried. It wasn't an easy job. Rhys was burned badly by the lightning and his pyjamas were charred. He must have died instantly."

"Was there a fire after the lightning struck Mr. Stone?" Avery asked.

"No, just a broken window where lightning entered the turret."

"What happened next, Mr. Allen?"

"As I pried up the boards of the chicken house, I knew I was doing wrong, but the wind howled, the rain lashed against the window, and Caroline kept badgering me to hurry up. Finally, we got him away from the ferocious storm—buried, in his pyjamas, beneath the wooden floor.

"Caroline was hysterical and full of rage, ordering me not to call the police. She made me promise I wouldn't tell anyone what happened. I kept that promise. Now everything's come to light with the discovery of Rhys' skeleton. I'm glad all this is out in the open now. Rhys' ghost has haunted me for a long time—that's partly why I sold the house. Maybe it will go away now."

"Do you know where Mrs. Stone is?" asked Lombardi. "It would be helpful if we could authenticate your story."

Mr. Allen fidgeted in his chair as beads of perspiration formed on his forehead and rolled into the cavity above his eye. He sighed deeply.

"I see her occasionally, but I never know when she's coming or where she lives. Sometimes, a year goes by in between visits. She's very secretive and unstable, though she does have some lucid moments. When the twins and my great-nieces came to return my helmet the other day, Caroline was visiting me, but bolted out the back door when the children arrived. She scared the kids. They thought she was a witch. It wasn't one of her good days. She looked pretty wild. She'll be back again, I'm sure."

"Why does Caroline come to see you?" Avery asked.

"She's after the emeralds."

"What emeralds?" asked Avery, not letting on that he already knew about Mr. Stone's emerald collection.

"Rhys Stone hand-wrote his Last Will and Testament a few years before he died. I know that because he asked me to be the executor of his estate. In it, he set out the terms and conditions for dispersal of his assets, including his emerald collection and Neptune's valuable dog collar. When Rhys disappeared like everyone thought, no one could locate his will. Eventually, he was declared legally dead after fruitless searches for him. It was hard not to confess that he was accidentally killed and Caroline and I had buried him. She was adamant that we keep quiet.

"Despite our best efforts, we couldn't find any of the precious stones he kept in little sacks hidden around the house. Rhys never told me where they were hidden. He assumed I would know. Sometimes, Caroline went crazy tearing the place apart, looking for the gems. Then, she started accusing me of finding them and taking them. I never would have done that, believe me. I loved Caroline. To my knowledge, the emeralds in the pouches have never been found, nor has the will. Both must still be in the Eden's home."

Detective Lombardi lost his patience.

"Mr. Allen, the next time you see Caroline Stone, get her down to the station immediately. We need to speak to her. Do you understand? Are you sure you don't know where she lives?"

"I have no idea. I don't think anyone knows. The next time I see her, I'll be in touch."

"Let's hope it's sooner, rather than later," said Lombardi. "This interview is over."

Avery and Sullivan walked Mr. Allen to the door while Lombardi shook his head in disbelief.

CHAPTER NINETEEN

The girls were getting antsy about the bone they had hidden in their bedroom closet. Alice suggested maybe Nora could identify it for them. "She works at the museum and sees bones all the time. Why don't we ask her?"

Emma grinned and opened her eyes wide. "That's a great idea. The police are taking their time finding out what Murphy's bone is. I have a feeling that it has something to do with the case. Ooh," she teased, "Maybe there's another skeleton somewhere."

Alice nodded her head slowly in agreement. "I've thought that all along. We can visit Nora after dinner when she has tea on her porch. I'm sure she'll help us."

When they had eaten, the twins ran upstairs to the closet and grabbed the bone from the shelf.

Murphy wagged his tail and yipped when Alice stuffed it in the canvas bag kept for his toys. They walked downstairs casually, not wanting to draw attention to themselves, and passed quietly by the door to the living room where their parents were reading the newspaper. "Where are you sneaking off to?" called Mum.

"We're just going out to swing and throw the ball for Murphy," Alice called back and kept walking. "Whew, that was close," she said quietly as they hurried out the door. "We'll tell Mum and Dad about our bone after Nora's looked at it. It would be nice if she could identify it and we could solve *that* mystery."

The twins skipped over to the swing to watch for Nora. "Good timing. She just stepped onto the porch. Hi, Nora," Alice called. "May we come for a quick visit? We have something to show you."

"Sure," answered Nora, "come on over." The twins opened the back gate and rushed up Nora's back stairs with Murphy. "What have you got there?" asked Nora when Alice playfully swung the dog's toy bag in front of her and pulled a bone out.

Nora's voice quivered. "A bone? Where on earth did you get that? A skeleton was just dug up, and now you're showing me a bone?"

"We found it on the front lawn," answered Emma, "after that spooky thunderstorm a while ago."

Alice turned and looked at Nora. "And we're the only ones who know about it."

"I'm baffled. Why didn't you tell anyone right away? Why the secret?"

"We didn't tell anyone about it because we wanted to find out what it was and where it came from ourselves. We've always wanted to be detectives and solve a mystery. Like Nancy Drew. We're sharing our secret with you."

"It wasn't the first bone that showed up," Emma added excitedly.

Nora raised her eyebrows in surprise and her eyes lit up. "What do you mean?"

Alice answered. "Murphy found one just like it a couple days *before* we found this one. Mum was really upset so Dad phoned the police and they came to pick it up, but we haven't heard anything yet."

"We hope you can tell us if this one's animal or human," Emma said breathlessly. "We're tired of keeping our secret. We want to tell Mum and Dad about it now and give it to the police."

Alice handed the bone to Nora. "We thought you'd be the best person to help us because you're an anthropologist and identify bones as part of your job."

Nora ran her fingers up and down the long bone, as though she were caressing it. "Bones are very interesting and tell us a story about their origins."

"Can you identify this bone, Nora?" asked Alice, impatiently.

"It's a tibia, from an animal. They look similar to a human tibia, but are smaller."

Alice and Emma looked at one another, eyes wide. "Thank you so much," said Alice. "This helps with the case. Now we can give the bone to the police and tell them we had it identified, by a professional. They will be very surprised."

"And pleased," added Emma. "We figure Mr. Stone's skeleton was more important to them, and they weren't really interested in the bone they took away."

Alice got up. "We should get home. We told Mum and Dad we were going to give Murphy some exercise in the back yard. They don't know we snuck over here first."

Emma tickled Murphy. "He knows we're going to play with him whenever we take his toy bag off the doorknob in our bedroom. Thanks for helping us. We'll play with Murphy for a while before we talk to Mum and Dad about the bone."

CHAPTER TWENTY

Y ou swing first, Emma. I'll throw the ball for Murphy. He hasn't had much playtime with all that's been going on lately."

Alice tossed the ball over to the cherry trees and Murphy ran lickety-split after it. A few seconds later, he dropped it into Alice's hand. Next, she threw the ball into the raspberry patch. While she waited, Emma jumped off the swing.

"Here, Alice, you have the swing now. I'll throw the ball." Alice grabbed the swing while Emma found Murphy nibbling raspberries.

"There you are, you little monkey, now come here and sit." Emma picked up the ball beside her and ran away with it. Before reaching the swing, she threw the ball high in the air. When it fell back to the ground it landed in the middle of the bramble patch which had flourished profusely due to the recent rainstorms. "Oh phooey, look where the ball's gone," she muttered. "Murphy, don't go in there...," she began when Murphy bounded into the thicket.

Try as they might, Alice and Emma couldn't coax him out. He wiggled this way and that, trying to forge a path through the prickly bushes. He was determined to find the ball. The girls heard him scrounging around in the underbrush which rustled and moved as he went deeper into the brambles.

Emma was worried. "I wish he'd come out. He's going to hurt himself. Those blackberry vines have awfully sharp thorns." Just then, Murphy let out a yip and began retracing his steps. When he emerged from the bushes he didn't have his ball. He was carrying a long bone, similar to the one he had dropped on the kitchen floor.

The girls managed to stifle a scream when Murphy dropped the bone into Alice's hands. "Gads. Another one. What is going on? Let's take it to Mum and Dad, right away. Things are getting too complicated. Ever since we moved here, it's been crazy. We'll show them our bone too and tell them what Nora said."

Emma nodded in agreement. "Good idea. I

don't think we should keep our secret any longer. Mum and Dad are going to be really mad. I'm scared."

"I'm scared too," admitted Alice as they headed back to the house. "First, let's deal with the one Murphy just found."

"Another bone? Where did you get this?" asked their stunned mother when the girls handed her a bone caked with dirt. Their father looked on speechless with thick furrowed eyebrows and stared at the twins. They knew that look—he wasn't happy.

"Murphy found it in the bramble patch behind the plum tree when he went to find his ball a few minutes ago. And here's another," said Alice calmly, withdrawing *their* bone from the canvas bag. "We found this one on the lawn after that thunderstorm two days *before* Murphy found the bone he dropped on the kitchen floor." She lowered her eyes. "We hid it in our cupboard."

"What? You two found a bone? Why didn't you tell us when you found it?" shouted Dad. "Why did you hide it? What were you thinking? You blew it."

"Now we have a third bone to deal with. This

is a nightmare!" their mother bellowed.

The twins had never seen their parents so upset. Emma sniffled, and felt a knot in her stomach, but managed to hold back tears. "We're really sorry. We wanted to solve the puzzle ourselves. We were getting tired of hiding the bone in our closet and wanted to get our secret over with, so we showed it to Nora after dinner today, seeing as how she works at the museum, and is an expert…" Emma began before her mother interrupted.

"Off to your room, both of you. Your father and I have to talk about this. Ugh," she groaned in disgust and threw up her hands.

"What's going to happen now, Alice?" asked Emma when the girls scurried up the stairs to their room. Murphy, who had cringed with fear when the tirade began, catapulted up the stairs after them. He curled up with the twins as they lay on their bed and wondered what to do next.

Alice groaned. "Well, we're in trouble for sure, and the investigators will come again, and there will be more digging, and the neighbours will *really* be wondering what's going on here. Constables Avery and Sullivan will be angry too.

That makes me sad. I really like them."

"I do too," said Emma. "It's too bad Mum wouldn't let us explain. We didn't even have a chance to say that the bone we found is from an animal. She was yelling too hard to listen. If only…," she sighed. "I bet the police will ID the bone they have at their lab pretty quick now. Do you think there's a skeleton in the bramble patch?"

Alice grinned. "I bet there is. What an awful muddle."

Just then, Murphy leapt off the bed when he heard a noise. He put his paws up on the windowsill and looked outside. The girls got up to see the police coming through the gate— Constables Avery and Sullivan, more investigators and more equipment.

A knock on their bedroom door startled them. It was their father. "You can come downstairs now, the police are here. They want to speak to you."

The twins, followed by their father and Murphy, went down to the kitchen to find their mother and a room full of police officers waiting for them.

Constable Avery looked stern and stood stiffly. "What's this about you finding a bone this evening?"

Alice spoke first in the cheeriest voice she could muster. "We were playing with Murphy and accidentally threw his ball into the brambles behind the plum tree. He crawled into the prickle bushes after it, but came out with a bone instead."

"Your father tells me that you found one too and hid it in your closet. So, now we have three to deal with—the first one which you found, the second which Murphy found and we took to the lab for identification, and this one which Murphy hauled out of the brambles today," Avery stated.

"Yes," the twins acknowledged sheepishly.

"You did the right thing by taking Murphy's new found bone to your parents right away, girls. But, hiding the first one in your closet was not a good idea. Concealing something which may become part of an investigation could be classed as a crime."

Alice's heart raced. "Even when it isn't human? The bone we found belongs to an animal. Nora just gave us the good news. It's not part of a human skeleton."

Avery was surprised. "Nora told you that?"

"Yes. She's an anthropologist and identifies all

sorts of things at the museum where she works, so we asked her if she would take a look at the bone we found. She knew right away that it was an animal's. We're learning a lot these days."

"We were really excited about that. Now Mum doesn't have to worry about someone being murdered here," said Emma as she smiled at her parents.

Their mother looked puzzled. "You didn't tell us all this."

"We tried to, but you yelled at us and told us to go to our room," said Alice.

The silence in the room was deafening. Avery broke the quietness when he spoke to the twins. "Well, no one has to worry about the bone we took away for analysis either. We've just had confirmation that it's animal too. Now, come and show us where the latest one turned up."

The twins grinned with relief as everyone trooped outside with Murphy leading the way. When Alice pointed to the spot, Murphy stood panting and moving his front feet up and down. "He came out with the bone right there. It was in the middle of the bramble patch."

"Maybe he found the first one there too,"

Emma whispered to Alice, as the police chatted and started unpacking their gear.

"I bet he did. I can hardly wait to see what they find," Alice whispered back.

The investigators closed off a wide section of property around the plum tree and the swing, and began the methodical job of clearing the brush from the outside in. Avery looked serious. "Be sure to keep your distance. And watch Murphy, girls. If there are more bones here, we don't want any interference." Alice and Emma stood silent, watching and waiting for something to happen.

When the girls saw Nora on her porch, they waved at her to join them. Keeping secrets wasn't as exciting as they thought.

Nora hurried up the lane and was met by Alice and Emma who gave her a quick rundown of what had happened. "They're looking for more. That's why they're ripping out the blackberries," said Emma. "We're all wondering what's in there."

"Good heavens," Nora moaned. "I'm flabbergasted that all this has turned up. And to think that all these years while living next door, I had no inkling that this beautiful place was practically a cemetery."

After the investigators had cleared the perimeter, they worked their way toward the centre of the brambles. Inch by inch they cleared away the brush and weeds, twisted ivy vines and old bits of wooden fencing, searching diligently for anything which could lead them to a crucial discovery.

"Careful. I think I see something." The lead investigator carefully moved the dirt aside. "Yes. There. It looks skeletal." Another man took samples of surrounding soil and debris as the unearthing continued.

"It's a bone alright. And, there's another." Everyone got as close to the spot as they could and craned their necks to get a better glimpse of what was being uncovered. The investigators moved with precision and revealed one bone after another.

"What's this? Four legs? What on earth has been buried here?" The investigator was clearly shocked.

Finally, a rib cage, long neck and large skull were unearthed. The onlookers gasped in horror.

Avery leaned closer toward the remains. "What's that, around the neck?"

"Looks like it could be a restraint, maybe. I think that's a buckle," advised an investigator, as he brushed some dirt away.

"But, what are those things there, covered in dirt?" Avery pointed to the distinct protrusions which were attached to the dark-coloured band encircling the skeleton's neck. As more dirt was removed, and the bulges began to take shape, Nora drew a deep breath and steadied herself when a fading beam of sunlight flickered through a branch of the plum tree and revealed a sudden flash of green.

"They're emeralds! It's Neptune, and that's his dog collar," screamed Nora who started to sob uncontrollably.

The twins cried too, and so did their mother who hugged her daughters tightly. Everyone was moved. It was a horrifying scene.

With twilight fast approaching, the site was secured for the night and everyone left. Nora dabbed the tears from her reddened face and was grateful when Avery offered to accompany her home. Her energy was gone; it was all she could do to climb the back stairs. The twins retreated to their bedroom where they found Murphy waiting for them on their bed. They stroked his fur and hugged him closely, then gave him a kiss.

While Alice and Emma finally fell asleep with Murphy snuggled between them, Nora tossed and turned in her bed next door.

CHAPTER TWENTY-ONE

The next day, when Avery and Sullivan returned to the scene to check on things, they encountered Nora and the twins, looking shell-shocked, in the back yard. Nora was at her wit's end.

"I'm mad as hell," she railed. "For almost twenty-two years I wondered what happened to Rhys Stone. He hadn't gone anywhere. He was here, all the time, lying in the dirt beneath the floor of his chicken house." She flung her arms in the air, and gestured toward the coop. "It's heart wrenching.

"He was a surrogate father to me and treated me just like his own daughter after he heard my father had been killed overseas. He often helped my mother with finances. Years later, when Heather became ill and died, he continued to keep me under his wing and paid for my university education through a trust fund."

Avery and Sullivan listened intently, not wanting to interrupt her, while the twins looked on with sympathetic frowns. Nora hadn't finished her rant.

"Neptune disappeared a year before Rhys did, and I always questioned the dog's fate. He wasn't stolen, he hadn't wandered away. *He* was buried in the garden where Heather and I played with him. Who buried him? And who buried Mr. Stone? All this is just so awful." She hung her head and cried softly.

"Everyone's working hard to solve this perplexing case, believe me. We know that nothing we say will bring you comfort, but we're doing everything possible to find answers to your questions," Avery said sympathetically, knowing he had the answer to one of her questions, but was holding back until all the pieces of the puzzle had come together.

Early that evening, when things had settled down,

Alice and Emma searched the turret for the emeralds. They discovered maps, yellowed with age, stuffed into weathered oak barrels and cubby holes in the walls. Some were marked with trade routes and notable ports of call along the coasts of North and South America and the South Sea islands. Others featured black ink sketches of whales with blowhole spray pinpointing the location of successful whale hunts. In a desk, they found old papers and sketch books filled with pencil drawings of sailing ships, whale encounters and stormy seas.

"Run your fingers underneath the drawers, Emma. See if you can find something tucked there—a letter maybe, or a sack of emeralds. Mr. Stone must have hidden something in the turret over the years. It's the perfect spot to hide a lot of things. I'll check the walls and see if there's a niche where something could be concealed. Like the spot we found downstairs for our Cracker Jack charms. We like to keep our treasures secret. I'm sure Mr. Stone kept a lot of things secret."

Emma sulked when she ran her fingers beneath and alongside the desk drawers. "Nothing's here, except slivers. I've got one in my little finger. It hurts."

"Keep looking," said Alice, who was busy feeling her way along the crevices between the cubby holes in the wall. "I know there's something important here. We just haven't found it yet."

Suddenly, the girls frantic searching was interrupted when their mother called from the kitchen. "Time to come downstairs, girls. Dinner's ready. Your father's home."

"Drats," Alice complained. "Right when we're in the middle of something, it's time to eat."

"We can come back after dinner, and look some more then," suggested Emma. "We don't want Mum to get annoyed at us again and keep dinner waiting."

"You're right. We're coming, Mum. Be right there," Alice yelled. "We'll find what we're searching for, I know it," said Alice, while they both put things away.

"What could it be?"

"Well, emeralds for sure. There must be other things too. We'll know what's important when we find it," Alice said confidently.

"What were you girls doing in the turret?" asked Mum when everyone sat down at the table.

"Just looking at old stuff belonging to the sea captain. Alice and I like the telescope best, but we also love the oil painting of Neptune with his collar and Mr. Stone with his curly white hair and bushy beard. Lizzy and Marie said that everything had been left in the turret for the new owners when their great-uncle sold the house. We think it's weird though, that the picture is still here."

Mum laughed. "That was nice of Mr. Allen. The telescope and all the other paraphernalia, including the picture, wouldn't look as nice without a turret to keep them in."

"I'll take a better look at the charts and instruments soon," mumbled Dad, who was enjoying his shepherd's pie.

The girls exchanged a worried look and finished their dinner quickly, hoping to continue their quest before their father went to investigate.

"No dessert? I've made chocolate cake."

"Maybe later," said Alice and Emma who were already heading upstairs.

Murphy wagged his tail and looked at the twins anxiously when they started their hunt again. "We'll walk you soon," said Alice. "We have a few more places to explore first."

On careful examination of the carved circular oak stand which supported the telescope, the girls found a slit near its base, just below one of the medallion-shaped pieces of wood which encircled the stand. The decoration closest to the opening was different from the others; it had a small indentation in the centre. Alice touched the dent gingerly with her forefinger then pushed it. Suddenly, a thin piece of wood, shaped like a tray, emerged from within. Resting on top was an envelope fastened with a glob of sealing wax imprinted with a sailing ship.

Alice gasped. "We found it. This is what we've been looking for."

Emma stood wide-eyed, wondering. "What is?"

"An important document, I think. We can open it when we take Murphy for his walk." Alice tucked the envelope into her pocket, and then pressed the wooden button which returned the tray to its hiding place.

The twins hurried downstairs and peeked into the kitchen. "We're taking Murphy for his walk now," Alice called. "We're going to visit Nora on the way home, but we shouldn't be too long."

"Have fun. We'll see you later."

CHAPTER TWENTY-TWO

The twins took Murphy down the back lane and up a few blocks to the park where they sat on a bench and watched him romp with the other dogs on the freshly mowed grass. Alice couldn't sit still. "I'm so excited I'm shaking."

Emma was fidgety too. "Hurry and open it. I can't stand the suspense."

Alice withdrew the treasure from her pocket and carefully pried the seal from the aged envelope without tearing it. Inside was a document handwritten in black ink. "It's a letter, signed by Rhys Stone and dated August 24, 1928. Let's take it back to Nora so she can read it with us," Alice said, eager to share what they had found.

The girls ran toward home with Murphy as fast as they could. When they reached Nora's, they saw her weeding in the vegetable garden and said hello.

Nora looked up. "Hi, girls. Come and join me for a cup of tea, and bring Murphy. I was just about to have a break."

"We were hoping you'd be home. Emma and I have two serious things that we want to talk to you about right now."

Nora removed her gardening gloves. "I'm all ears."

The girls unlatched the back gate and followed Nora into the kitchen where she made tea and got dog treats for Murphy. "Let's sit on the porch. What's up?"

Alice and Emma began with news of their visit to Rex Allen's house to return the army helmet they found beneath the front stairs.

"I'm sure he was glad to have it back," said Nora. "I first saw it when he came to speak at our high school on Remembrance Day in my senior year. Given his severe head wound, he was lucky to have survived."

"We went to his place with Lizzy and Marie and just before we got there, something weird happened," said Emma. "A witch ran out the back door and disappeared down the lane. She scared all of us so much that we were afraid to go inside his house."

"A witch? Really? Did Mr. Allen say who it was?"

"No. He just said she was a friend and we had nothing to worry about. I can't imagine anyone having a friend like that," said Emma with her nose wrinkled in disgust.

"After we gave him the helmet, we went home and told Constables Avery and Sullivan all about it, just before they interviewed Mr. and Mrs. McTavish. We told them they should stake out Mr. Allen's place. There's something fishy about the witch," Alice said breathlessly.

"What did she look like?" Nora asked.

"Well, she didn't wear a black witch's hat if that's what you were thinking," said Emma. "She was really unkempt. We couldn't see what she was wearing because she was fully covered by a long flowing black coat. It was really hot outside too. We all had shorts on."

"We have something else to tell you," said Alice who was itching to tell Nora about the letter. "It's very, very important."

"Okay, what is it?"

"We found a letter in the turret that was written

by Mr. Stone. Alice reached into her pocket and gave the envelope to Nora who immediately opened it and read out loud. Her voice became softer and more hesitant while she spoke.

I, Rhys Stone, being of sound mind and body, declare that this document be construed as my last Will and Testament. I bequeath the following as noted and appoint Rex Allen to act as Executor of my Estate to distribute such items upon my death.

1. *To my wife, Caroline Stone, I leave my home, furniture and artwork, my bank accounts, investments, and vehicle for her own use or to sell at her discretion.*

2. *To my wife, Caroline Stone, I leave my emerald collection to use or sell at her discretion, subject to the following conditions:- (i) Rex Allen, my friend and Executor, will act as trustee of my emerald collection and distribute the emeralds as follows, (ii) On the first of December each year after my death, Rex Allen will provide my wife, Caroline Stone, with one pouch containing six emeralds only, until all six pouches containing six emeralds each,*

have been distributed and the supply of emeralds is exhausted, (iii) If my wife, Caroline Stone should die before all six pouches have been distributed, the remainder of the pouches, complete with emeralds, become the sole property of Rex Allen upon her death.

3. *In lieu of my daughter, Heather, who died when she was a child, I leave the emerald dog collar, hand tooled for my beloved dog, Neptune, to my neighbour, Nora Stevenson, to keep or sell at her discretion, with the following conditions,(i) My wife, Caroline Stone, cannot contest the emerald dog collar bequest, (ii) If she does so, either in writing, by legal challenge, or otherwise, her bequest of six pouches containing six emeralds each, will be rescinded, and Rex Allen will immediately become the beneficiary of all said pouches and emeralds.*

4. *Let it be known that Neptune died of natural causes on July 26, 1928. I, Rhys Stone, buried him on the family property, behind the plum tree, where Neptune's*

emerald collar can be found, buried with him.

Signed: Rhys Stone, August 24, 1928

Witness: Thomas McTavish, August 24, 1928

After reading the document, Nora's face paled. She lost her grip on the paper which floated to the floor. "I'm astonished. Whew. I'm feeling a little lightheaded." Alice bent over, picked it up, and returned it to her pocket.

"Are you okay?" asked Emma while Alice got her a glass of cold water.

"Yes, I'm fine, just shocked." Nora took a drink and was suddenly full of questions. "Neptune's disappearance has been explained, but why was it kept a secret? He died of natural causes. Why didn't Mr. Stone advise us that his dog had died? And why was he buried with his valuable collar on? His decision to leave the emerald collar to me is unbelievable." She began to cry softly, remembering the giant dog that had captured her heart.

"Finding the letter was a big surprise," said Alice hoping to ease Nora's sorrow. "It was hidden in the telescope stand. We wanted to show it to you first. We have to tell our parents about it, and give it to the police right away."

"Yes," said Nora, who regained her composure. "Yes, you do."

Emma was moved by Nora's uneasiness. "Are you sad, Nora?"

"Yes, it brings back a lot of memories. But, I'm relieved to know that Neptune wasn't stolen and that Mr. Stone buried him when he died. It brings me peace, in a way. We're so lucky that Murphy found that bone and alerted us to Neptune's burial site. But, let's forget about sorrow. Your concern touches me deeply. Let's drink our tea, before it gets cold, then you can go home and give the will to your parents."

As they sipped their tea and Murphy lay dozing at their feet, the twins wanted to know more about Nora's friend.

"What happened to Heather when she died?" asked Alice.

"Well, when Heather passed away her parents had a funeral for her in St. Martin's Anglican church not far from here. That was a long time ago, in 1926. My mother and I attended, along with a few of the neighbours, including Mr. and Mrs. McTavish, and some friends of the Stone family.

They didn't have any relatives here.

"After the funeral we all went to the North Vancouver Cemetery for her burial. I cried my eyes out when they put her casket in the grave. Neptune, bless his heart, stood close beside me wondering what was going on. He looked sad and whined softly when they shovelled earth onto the casket. Afterwards, the Stones had a nice tea party beneath the plum tree to honour their daughter, and everybody came. But, it wasn't the same without Heather.

"You know, I just had a thought. It sounds eerie, but I think it's respectful, and given all the commotion around here, it would bring a great deal of closure and comfort to some of us. I know it would mean a lot to me."

"What?" asked the twins.

"Well, when the police have finished examining Mr. Stone's and Neptune's bones, I wonder if they'd consider having them cremated so that their ashes could be buried beside Heather in the cemetery. Heather's gravesite is marked with a pretty marble headstone engraved with her name. Perhaps we can go to the cemetery and find it sometime."

"I think that would be nice to see Heather's gravesite," Alice added, "and it sounds like a good place for Mr. Stone's and Neptune's remains."

"We'll go for a visit soon," Nora suggested, "but I just thought of something. I don't know if the city would allow Neptune's ashes to be buried at the cemetery." Her frown quickly changed to a smirk when she said, "Let's not worry about that. I'm sure Constables Avery and Sullivan could get around that if they tried. It could be *their* secret," she smiled, looking over at Alice and Emma. Her brown eyes sparkled. "Do you think policemen have secrets?"

"I bet they do. Mr. Stone had secrets. Sometimes we have secrets, but they don't always work out," Alice said, seriously.

Their parents were in the sunroom reading when the twins got home. "Back already?" asked Mum. "You weren't very long. I thought you were going to visit Nora."

"We did," answered Alice. "But we were in a hurry to get home and show you what we found in the turret. It's a letter written by Mr. Stone before he died."

"It's really old," Emma added excitedly when she and Alice gave the envelope with its special seal to their parents.

Dad was dumbfounded. "How interesting. Where did you find it?" Before the girls could answer, Mum read the document aloud, raising and lowering her eyebrows with each line.

"It's Mr. Stone's will. It answers some questions, but poses others. Neptune never was missing, and thanks to Murphy, he's been found, exactly where Mr. Stone confessed to burying him. Now the emerald collar has been discovered, it will be given to Nora one day, according to Mr. Stone's wishes. I'm happy for her. But, I'm curious about Caroline. Whatever happened to her? We'll pass this on to the police right away. It will help with the investigation."

"They're going to be very excited, that's for sure. And to answer your question, Dad, it was hidden in a secret compartment near the bottom of the telescope stand in the turret," said Alice.

"All those emeralds. Just imagine," Dad pondered. "Since the will has just been discovered,

I wonder what happened when Mr. Stone disappeared. Did his wife ever get the emeralds? Rex Allen and Thomas McTavish will be surprised to hear it's turned up. And, Nora must have been surprised to learn she has inherited Neptune's collar. That dog meant so much to her. The police really have their work cut out for them this time."

Mum got up from her chair and placed the envelope on the tea wagon beside her. "Good work, girls. Constables Avery and Sullivan will be stunned at what you've found. Another piece of the puzzle has come to light, but I'm sure there's more to come. Thanks for showing us the will when you found it. No more secrets, right? Now, have a piece of your favourite cake."

After dessert and a glass of milk, the girls went up to their room and read before settling down for the night. "Mum and Dad are in a really good mood," said Emma. "Thank goodness they're not upset with us anymore."

CHAPTER TWENTY-THREE

Avery and Sullivan arrived at the Eden residence just before nine the next morning. Alice and Emma giggled when they handed them the envelope. "A gift for you, just what you wanted," said Emma.

"More evidence." Alice was so excited she was wriggling, something which Granny had always referred to as St. Vitus' dance when she couldn't stay still.

As the constables unfolded the envelope and read the will, the girls told them the story of how they had found it in the turret when they pressed a little wooden decoration on the telescope stand.

"It just popped right out. There it was, inside the old envelope stamped with a beautiful sailing ship in a wax seal to keep it safe. It's very old and the handwriting is different. Are you pleased we found it?" Alice teased.

"We're thrilled. Thanks again, girls, for a job well done. There's no doubt you've done the work of two extra police officers this last little while," said Avery. "This is a lucky find."

A grin lit up Sullivan's face. "Lombardi's going to be very pleased with this."

When the officers left, Alice said, "Let's go over to Mr. Allen's place and see if the witch is there again. We can hide behind the hedge and wait."

"I don't know," Emma scowled. "She was awfully scary."

"It will be alright. We can ask Lizzy and Marie to come with us. Afterwards, we could go to Mahon Pool for a swim."

Emma quickly changed her mind. "A swim sounds great."

"We're going right by your Great-Uncle Rex's house on the way to pool, so let's stop there first and see if the witch is around," Alice told Lizzy and Marie when they met them. "We can go down the alley and park our bikes, then peek through the hedge."

"Why not?" said Marie.

From their hiding place the girls could see clearly into the living room through little spaces in the greenery. "There's great-uncle," said Lizzy "and he's carrying something...his army helmet, I think, and he's showing it to someone getting up from the sofa. I think it is Caroline Stone, all dressed up. She looks just like the picture of her that great-uncle kept on his desk. She still wears her hair tied back with a ribbon."

"I remember that picture. It *is* her," said Marie. "They're arguing. Look. She just pushed great-uncle. She's yelling and seems really mad about something." The girls kept quiet and listened to the raised voices coming through the open window.

"What do you mean the police want to see me?" shouted Caroline. "What do they want with me?"

"It's about Rhys. They found his skeleton in the chicken coop and..."

Caroline interrupted him. "What do you mean? Rhys is dead? I wondered where he was. I've been looking for him. What happened to him?"

"You don't recall the thunderstorm and the lightning that killed him? Please say you remember that horrible night when we buried him," Mr. Allen pleaded.

"I have no idea what you're talking about. I'm looking for the emeralds. I can't find them. Do you know where they are?"

"I have no idea. Where are you living? You're not well, Caroline. Please come to the police station with me. We can help you," Mr. Allen begged.

The girls were frightened by the arguing and loud voices. "We must tell the police about this, right away," said Alice.

"I can't believe what great-uncle said. Mr. Stone wasn't murdered. That's good. But, he buried Mr. Stone in the chicken coop? That's awful. Forget about swimming. I'm too upset to go," said Lizzy with disgust.

The girls pedalled home as fast as they could. Alice and Emma told their mother what they had seen and heard. "We're going to the police station to tell the constables right now. We just wanted to let you know where we're going," said Alice. Alice and Emma jumped back on their bikes, and took off.

"Come right home, afterwards," their mother called after them. "I worry about you both."

When they got there, Avery and Sullivan were flipping through their note books in the parking lot.

Alice was out of breath. "I'm glad we found you. We were staking out Mr. Allen's place and we saw and heard him arguing with Mrs. Stone through an open living room window."

"Wait a minute," said Avery, puzzled. "What do you mean you saw Mrs. Stone?"

"We were with Lizzy and Marie and they recognized her," said Emma. "Mr. Allen was talking about Mr. Stone and the lightning that killed him. He asked Mrs. Stone if she remembered the night they buried him. She said no. She thinks he's still alive."

"Mrs. Stone is looking for the emeralds, but she didn't say where," Alice said. "I think you better get over there quick."

Avery was stunned. "Thanks. We'll get right on it." He and Sullivan scrambled into their vehicle and headed for Mr. Allen's home, without the siren, but the witch was nowhere to be found.

CHAPTER TWENTY-FOUR

H ow would you like to spend the day with me tomorrow?" proposed Nora that evening. I have something special in mind. It's okay with your parents."

"What is it?" asked the twins.

"The Pacific National Exhibition. We can go on the Ferris wheel, the roller coaster, the Tilt a Whirl and tons of other rides, and visit the farm animals in the 4H exhibits. There's interesting stuff to see in the exhibition halls, and plenty of goodies to eat, like cotton candy and…"

"We'd love to go! Lizzie and Marie told us all about the PNE," said Emma.

"Can we get one of those big stuffed animals?" asked Alice.

"If you're good at knocking targets over with a ball. Who was it that accidentally threw the ball into the brambles?" The three of them laughed when Alice and Emma poked fingers at one another.

"We'll go early, when the gate opens. Be sure to wear your saddle shoes."

The twins retired early that evening. After reading a chapter from their latest Nancy Drew novel, they jumped into bed full of anticipation. Murphy was already curled up fast asleep on his mat. A full moon lit up the star-studded sky; there wasn't a storm cloud in sight.

In the middle of the night, Alice and Emma were jolted awake when Murphy jumped onto their bed whining and frantically licking their faces. Alice turned on the bedside lamp and squinted at the clock. "It's 3:00am, Murphy. Go back to sleep." Murphy nudged her chin, and then tugged on her pyjama sleeve. "Okay, okay, do you have to pee? We'll take you outside. Hold your horses."

The girls stumbled out of bed and put on their dressing gowns. Murphy ran to the moonlit bedroom closet and stopped under the window. He pricked his ears and whined. A rhythmic metallic noise was coming from outside. Alice pushed the window open and thrust her head into the cool night air to see what it was.

"Someone's climbing up the fire escape to the turret," she whispered. "I think it's the witch."

Emma peered out the window and couldn't believe what she saw. Someone *was* climbing up the stairs to the turret. Someone wearing a long black coat. Murphy barked ferociously. A bone-chilling scream arose from the figure when it suddenly stumbled and fell from the top step to the grass below.

The girls jumped into their slippers, and flew downstairs to alert their parents. "What's all that barking about?" Dad yelled, rushing out of the bedroom.

"Did I hear somebody scream?" Mum murmured, rubbing her eyes.

"Somebody was climbing up the fire escape to the turret. Then they fell off the top step," sobbed Alice. Emma whimpered beside her. Everyone was frozen in shock for a moment before they rushed outside.

The full moon illuminated the area where the body landed. Dad was first to reach the prone figure and check for life signs. "She's alive, but barely breathing."

"I'll call Constable Avery's emergency number right away," yelled Mum when she saw the body. "He said it was okay to call him after hours if we needed him. I'll grab a blanket too."

Alice and Emma were hesitant about approaching the body. Their stomachs churned and they shook from shock. "Let's see if it's you-know-who," whispered Emma. Alice nodded, and the girls clung to one another as they slowly crept to where the body lay. They recognized the long black coat, but what did the face look like? They were afraid to look. Suddenly, the head moved to look at them, and a wheezing sound came from its lips. The girls screamed in terror. It was Mrs. Stone, dressed as the witch.

"Where... are the...emeralds?" a feeble and raspy voice asked, before letting out a long and final sigh.

"She's passed away," said Dad quietly after

checking the woman's pulse. Alice and Emma sobbed as their mother covered the body with a blanket.

Minutes later, sirens echoed through the night, growing louder as emergency vehicles approached the Eden residence. By the time police and a doctor arrived, neighbours were gathered in the street. Avery immediately dispersed the crowd, except for Nora who rushed over from next door to find chaos again.

"Are you okay, girls?" Nora asked Alice and Emma who were shaking and clutching their dressing gowns tightly around them as they stared at the corpse. "What happened?"

In between sobs and hiccups, Alice managed to answer their friend. "Murphy was barking, and we looked out our window and saw someone fall off the fire escape."

"That's Caroline Stone lying there, dead," said Nora, looking at the crumpled body. "I hardly recognize her in that getup. What on earth was she doing climbing the fire escape in the middle of the night?" Nora's face was twisted and tears fell from her eyes as she bent over and held her stomach. "I feel sick."

After the doctor formally pronounced the accident victim dead and photographs had been taken, interviews were concluded and the body was taken away.

"What a tragedy," Avery sighed. He seemed tired and moved by the traumatic death of Mrs. Stone and upset that Alice and Emma had witnessed the horrific event. "Get to bed now girls. You need to sleep. We'll talk tomorrow. You've had enough shocks over the last few weeks to last a lifetime."

"We had plans to go to the PNE with Nora tomorrow, but I don't want to go now," Alice sniffled, her face streaked with tears.

"I don't want to go anywhere," Emma sobbed. "I'm too sad. Like when Granny died."

"It's been a sad and disturbing night for all of us," said Nora, traumatized herself by Mrs. Stone's accidental demise. "I agree, sleep is what we all need. We can go to the PNE another day." She hugged the girls and left, weeping as she made her way home with Avery by her side.

"Let's get to bed now," said Mum, whose face was puffy and red from sobbing after she and her husband finished speaking to investigators. Alice and Emma embraced their parents, and walked slowly into the house arm in arm. Murphy, waiting by the door, licked away their tears and led them upstairs to bed.

CHAPTER TWENTY-FIVE

Nora popped over to see the girls after breakfast the next day. "How are you?" she asked.

"I'm feeling sad." Emma frowned and sighed. "Poor Mrs. Stone. It was a dreadful way to die. I still can't believe it really happened."

"It was such a strange accident," said Alice. "I'm sorry that Mrs. Stone was so distressed. It's a shame someone couldn't have helped her with her problems. She didn't have to die."

"I'm deeply saddened by her death too. Before Heather passed away, her mother was a very different and warm person. She loved life. When Heather died all that changed. Grief consumed her and she never got over it. The loss of Neptune and Mr. Stone was the final straw. None of us knew who she was anymore. Now that she's gone, I want to honour her memory."

Emma smiled. "That would be nice. It would make us all feel better. What do you want to do?"

"I've talked to Constable Avery regarding arrangements for Mrs. Stone. After cremation, her ashes can be buried with Mr. Stone and Neptune at Heather's gravesite. Why don't we visit the cemetery and find Heather's resting place now? You can get an idea of where the service will be held, and help me choose flowers for the burial spot. Would you like that?"

"Yes, very much," said Alice and Emma.

When they found Heather's headstone and saw the beautiful forest with its different shades of green surrounding the cemetery, Alice and Emma had suggestions. "How about bouquets of heather, white English roses and fragrant freesias?" Alice proposed.

"Tied with vibrant green ribbons," added Emma. "Granny loved English roses, they're so pretty, and Mum had freesias in her wedding bouquet. And mauve heather would be for Heather.

I bet she was named after the plant."

"She was," said Nora. "Those are wonderful ideas."

CHAPTER TWENTY-SIX

T he back yard is yours again, so you can get your paint brushes ready," Avery told the twins when he and Sullivan dropped by to chat with their parents about the latest developments involving the accidental death of Caroline Stone. "You should be able to meet your deadline and get the library completed before school starts."

"Goody," said Emma. "Can we start today, Dad? Alice and I will get everything ready. Then we can start painting. We'll help you with the new floor and we can wash the windows when everything's done."

Alice looked at her father. "We'll work really hard, I promise. Maybe Lizzy and Marie can help us. They're just as excited as we are."

"We're too busy to talk about it now. Why

164

don't you take Murphy for some exercise?" Dad suggested.

"That sounds like a good idea," said Sullivan. "Things will be back to normal soon."

"We don't know what normal is anymore," said Alice matter-of-factly. "Finding bones and skeletons isn't normal. After all this, maybe normal will be boring."

"Well, at least we'll be starting school soon," said Emma. "That will keep us busy and we'll have lots of tales to tell our new friends."

When the girls left with Murphy who carried a new red ball, Avery and Sullivan began their update involving the fire escape incident.

"Caroline Stone's accidental fall and subsequent demise, tragic as it was, has fast-tracked the case," announced Avery. "As you know, we wanted to interview her about her husband's death to validate what Rex Allen told us, but now that's impossible. So, we'll have to proceed with what we have. As far as we know, there weren't any witnesses to the lightning strike that killed Rhys Stone. The McTavishes didn't see anything. They slept through most of the storm.

"We've been in constant meetings with

Detective Lombardi. It's still up in the air if any charges will be laid against Mr. Allen for interfering with a dead body when he buried Mr. Stone in the chicken coop."

"Then, there's the matter of the will the girls found," Sullivan said. "Since Rhys Stone was declared dead a long time ago, and some of his assets have already been distributed, that's not a concern. However, the matter of the missing emeralds is problematic. It's a very unusual situation, but I'm sure the lawyers will work everything out, once the emeralds are located."

"The fact that Caroline Stone asked the twins where the emeralds were while she lay dying, leads us to believe that the gems are somewhere in your home, and that was the reason she was scaling the fire escape. We'll have to undertake a search for them. Sullivan and I can come by tomorrow morning."

"Good. The girls will be pleased to help with the search," said their mother.

CHAPTER TWENTY-SEVEN

The police were gone by the time Alice and Emma returned with Murphy who was tuckered out from chasing the ball up and down the grassy knolls at the park.

"The constables left a while ago," said Mum. "They'll be by again tomorrow to search for Mr. Stone's missing emeralds."

"We've got to find the emeralds first," Alice said to Emma when they ran upstairs to their room. "It's going to be a test of our detective skills against the police. We've got to keep one step ahead of them. We've learned a lot from Nancy Drew. Let's get busy. We'll look in the turret again."

Emma agreed. "If we don't have any luck there, we can search the passageway between the sunroom and the piano room where we stashed our

Cracker Jack charm collection. Maybe we'll find another hidey-hole."

Murphy pricked up his ears when he heard the word turret and followed the girls up the closet stairway. He soon regained his energy and ran around the room where the telescope and other curiosities were kept.

"He sure is excited," Emma said as the girls began searching for the gems. "He's going crazy. Maybe he's thinking about the accident."

"Go and lie on your mat. No one's here," Alice told the dog who was running in circles and getting in their way. "Settle down."

Murphy ran to his mat, jumped onto it and was about to lie down when the mat slid on the slippery polished floor and skidded across the room. Despite hanging on for dear life, he lost his footing, flew off the mat and collided with one of the old wooden barrels which held some maps. The barrel spun over to the far wall where it crashed and spilled its contents, while the metal rim on the bottom flew off in another direction.

"Oh no, the barrel is broken," Emma cried as Murphy took off down the staircase and hid underneath the girls' bed. After checking to make sure he wasn't injured, Emma returned to the turret and helped Alice collect the maps and lean them against a corner wall.

"Maybe we can fix it," said Alice. When they attempted to re-attach the metal rim, they noticed that the wood at the base of the barrel was cracked and wobbly. Alice pushed on the wood and it gave way. Suddenly, two little sacks fell out of a false bottom. Trying hard to keep their composure, the twins grabbed a sack each, undid the ties, and dumped a dozen shimmering green emeralds onto the floor.

Screams of joy echoed throughout the house. Mum rushed up from the kitchen, Murphy returned to the turret and began barking, and the girls started crying. "We found them. We did it," sobbed Alice. "We actually found some emeralds. Now we've got to find the rest."

When the girls told their mother that Murphy helped them find the emeralds because he accidentally crashed into the barrel, she was astounded.

"I'm amazed. Just look at these. What a find. Murphy is worth his weight in gold."

"Or emeralds," Alice said, jokingly. She patted

Murphy on the head and tickled his ears. "Good boy."

"According to the will, there are four more sacks waiting to be discovered somewhere in the house," reminded Emma.

Alice was deep in thought. "If they haven't been found already. But, I have a strong feeling the rest of them are here hiding, just waiting for us to find them. That's why the witch, I mean Mrs. Stone, was climbing the fire escape in the middle of the night. She remembered the emeralds were here. She may have been crazy, but she never forgot the precious stones. I don't think anybody could ever forget an emerald once they had seen one. Look how they shine. They're just like the stars in the sky, except they're green instead of white."

Mum ran her fingers across each of the emeralds and picked up the largest gem to marvel at its clarity and rich, sea green colour before she and the twins put the emeralds back into two sacks, six emeralds in each one, just like Mr. Stone had done before he secreted them away.

"I'll put them in the cookie jar to keep them safe until the constables come to search for more.

They can take these away for safekeeping like Neptune's emerald collar."

Alice and Emma searched the passageway next. The deep drawers were filled with odds and ends like candles and vases, old photograph albums, and autograph books. "Our Cracker Jacks charms are still safe in their hidey-hole, but there's nowhere else to hide anything here," said Emma. "Let's look at the top of the drawers."

The girls needed a step stool to peek into the narrow top drawer which almost reached the cove ceiling. It was reserved for Granny's elegant antique jewelry which their mother didn't wear often. An elaborate four piece set containing two necklaces, a bracelet and ring made with semi-precious garnets and gold, was kept in a leather and silk-lined box.

"Granny's old jewelry is pretty neat," crooned Alice.

"But garnets are not as beautiful as emeralds. Granny didn't have emeralds, but she had diamond rings. Now Mum wears them. I think they're as pretty as emeralds," Emma said.

"I'm going to look above the top drawer, in the little space just below the cove ceiling. It's a long reach, but I think I can make it," Alice said, after she and Emma took turns looking at Granny's treasures.

While standing tippy-toe on the top step, she found a tiny shelf. Alice moved her fingers slowly along the old wood ledge. "It's very dusty." Suddenly, she felt something. "Gads, there are dead spiders here and clingy spider webs." She shook her hand in disgust. "I hate the way they stick to your fingers. We'll get rid of them later."

Alice had almost come to the end of the cramped shelf when her fingers came across something soft. "It's fabric," she told Emma, excitedly. Her hands began to tremble as she eased the material forward. When it came free, she lost her balance and almost fell from the stool. When she saw the familiar fabric, she knew it was another gem sack, and hurriedly climbed down the steps so she and Emma could open it together.

"It's the same dark green brocade material, and the tie is identical, but...," Alice said as they unknotted the little sash and looked inside. "It's empty. The emeralds are gone."

Emma frowned. "Why would anyone put an empty sack back on the shelf? I don't get it. I bet

Mrs. Stone found it, scooped the emeralds, and put the sack back to fool Mr. Stone and make him think his gems were still there."

Alice was upset. "Maybe. But this is very frustrating. I was so excited when I felt the cloth. Now, I'm disappointed. We have to search again, after we've been to the PNE. I can't believe we're going with Nora tomorrow."

CHAPTER TWENTY-EIGHT

For the first time in weeks, the girls forgot about bones and skeletons and death. The PNE's exhibition buildings were packed with all sorts of things they had never seen before, and the midway rides were exhilarating.

"We haven't had so much fun in ages," Emma told Nora when she and Alice staggered off the Tilt a Whirl. "It's a good thing we didn't eat lunch before we went on the rides."

At the ball toss booth, the girls took turns trying to win a prize. In the end, it was Emma's shot that snagged a massive blue and white stuffed dog that was almost as tall as they were. Nora laughed as they hugged the plush toy. "Are you sure you can carry it home, girls?"

"We'll help each other," said Alice. "We wanted one of those prizes so badly."

After lunch at a hamburger booth Emma joked that she had never seen so many fried onions stuffed into a hamburger bun. "I'm full. Maybe we can get cotton candy on the way home."

The afternoon went by quickly. Nora suggested they should leave. "I told your parents we'd be home for dinner. First, let's take a ride on the roller coaster. It's the scariest ride here. We can scream our hearts out together."

When the trio arrived home, things were quiet. Murphy didn't run to greet them like he usually did. Mum and Dad weren't out in the garden either. Nora and the girls walked around to the back of the house. Nobody was there. They opened the back door to the kitchen and called out, but no one answered.

"Let's go upstairs and see if Mum and Dad are there. Maybe Murphy's asleep on our bed," said Alice. "Come with us, Nora. I'm worried."

When they opened the door to their bedroom, they almost fell backwards when their parents jumped out at them and yelled, "Surprise.

Surprise," then started to laugh. Murphy barked and wagged his tail and rushed over to greet them.

Alice and Emma screamed with excitement when they saw their room. The walls were covered with new wallpaper resplendent with sailing ships, a rolling blue ocean and billowing white clouds floating across a clear blue sky.

"Wow," the girls cried with happiness, and gave their parents a big hug. "Thank you so much."

"You fooled us. That's what you were doing all day. We would never have guessed. Now we won't have any more scary creatures staring at us when a thunderstorm comes," Emma said with tears in her eyes.

Alice's eyes were misty too. "It's the wallpaper from the hardware store, Nora. Isn't it beautiful?"

"It's lovely. Your parents told me all about it, so we devised a plan. I'd take you to the exhibition while they hung the wallpaper. I think it worked out well, don't you?"

"It sure did," echoed the twins. "It was a wonderful surprise."

"Please stay for dinner, Nora," said Mum. "We want to hear all about the PNE. And, we want to know what you girls did to win the stuffed dog that

Murphy's made friends with."

CHAPTER TWENTY-NINE

After a busy morning in the turret, Alice and Emma relaxed on the swing, stretching their legs and enjoying the warm breeze in their hair. Storm clouds formed quickly over the mountains behind them and thunder rumbled as a late afternoon storm advanced from the northeast. Dark clouds drifted across the sky, obscuring the sun, turning the day dark and foreboding. The twins retreated to their bedroom to contemplate their next move. Murphy wasn't happy when the thunder boomed and shook the house. He curled up on the mat beside their bed, put his paws over his ears, and trembled.

"Looks like we're in for another big one, but at least we don't have that creepy wallpaper anymore," Emma said when a big flash lit up their room. "I didn't see anything scary, no ghouls, just our beautiful new sailing ships. That's good. They're gone."

The rain came down in buckets as the storm intensified and the thunder and lightning continued. "Why don't we go outside like Mr. Allen suggested and have a gander at the turret and see if the ghost appears," Alice suggested.

"Okay," Emma agreed, "but let's leave Murphy inside. When the girls put on their raincoats, Murphy whimpered. "We're not going to be long, Murphy. Stay and mind the fort." Murphy crawled under the bed.

The twins hurried outside and stood in silence on the sidewalk near the front gate. They had a good view of the turret and focused their eyes on the telescope as they waited for the apparition to appear. Emma pouted. "He probably won't come because we're standing here looking."

The wind picked up and buffeted everything in its path. Tree branches bent and danced in the wind. The whale weathervane spun on its axis and changed direction every time the wind did. The twins shivered in the chilly, unrelenting rain.

"He'll come, I know it. Keep your eyes focused on the telescope, Emma. If he's going to be anywhere, he'll be there. Get ready for the next bolt of lightning."

Time passed. The rain continued to fall, but the lightning and thunder had abated. The twins were about to go inside when a big bolt of lightning lit up the turret like a powerful searchlight.

"Wow," Alice shouted when she spotted the ghost staring at them while he rested one hand on top of the telescope to support his shimmering frame. Her heart raced, her body trembled, and her voice squeaked. "Did you see him, Emma?"

"Yes. I'm quivering all over. So, that's what a real ghost looks like."

Alice was ecstatic. "The ghost is still living here. He really exists, like everybody said. And now we've seen him. We are so lucky. Let's go inside. I'm getting cold."

The storm had moved on by the time the twins dried off and decided what to do next. "Okay. Let's make one more search of the turret and see if we can find any more emeralds. If not, I'm sure the police will locate something. They're the ones with the expertise, but we're getting pretty good at finding things. It's been fun, hasn't it, Emma?"

"It sure has. I'm going to miss seeing the

constables when all this is over. It really has been an interesting summer. I love all this detective stuff, skulking around and watching the investigators dig up bones. It's like we're in the middle of our own mystery book."

"They'll be here first thing tomorrow," reminded Alice. "Let's see what we can find before then."

Happy to be out of his hiding place, Murphy followed the girls when they went back to the turret. He curled up on his mat and put his head down when they began exploring again.

Alice pondered out loud. "What did we miss?" She looked around the room with its ample windows. There wasn't a lot of wall space. They had already checked all the cubby holes. Her eyes kept moving, and then stopped at the heavy brass bell strung up with a macramé cord. She turned the bell upside down, and looked past the knotted clapper pull. Nothing was hidden there.

"We've already looked at the bell," reminded Emma who stopped to admire the intricacy of the pattern again. She thought back to when Lizzy and Marie had given them a tell-tale tour of the turret and first told them about macramé. The girls fingered the work, wondering how anyone could tie knots so tightly that they formed a flawless, almost cloth-like piece of work. Though the knots were white, a hint of dark green, almost black could be seen beneath them.

Alice grinned. "I wonder what that coloured piece is. Do you think it's a sack of emeralds? The only way we can find out is to cut the knots apart. I don't think we should do that, but…"

"Let's do it, Alice. We can do it together, and if we get in trouble, we'll suffer together. It won't be the first time. And it won't be the last." The twins snickered.

"Okay. We'll cut the end knots of the clapper cord which won't ruin the rest of the knotting. That way we can cut just a few knots and see what's underneath. Is there a pair of scissors in the desk?"

Emma opened the top drawer and found what they needed. While she held the cord tightly in her fingers, her sister cut one knot after another. Three rows of knots had been cut all the way through before Alice could see what lay beneath. It wasn't hard like wood. It was soft, yet firm. She severed another row of knots and gently eased the fabric out of its hiding place.

"It's another sack of emeralds. I can feel them. Look, Emma," cried Alice while she gently held the treasure they had been searching for. "Mr. Stone was very clever. He put the emeralds in the brocade sack, rolled it up, and then covered it with macramé knots."

Alice and Emma untied the sash together and opened the pouch to find six more emeralds from Rhys Stone's collection.

"Only two more sacks to find," Alice said, overjoyed at what she and her sister had accomplished. "Let's call it a day. We'll let Constables Avery and Sullivan locate the rest."

Emma was doubtful. "Let's hope more stones are here."

"They're here, alright," Alice answered confidently, "but we need help getting them out of their hiding spot."

CHAPTER THIRTY

W e'll have to wait a few more days before painting the library," Emma said when she and Alice woke up early the next day. "Everything got a good soaking with all that rain yesterday." The girls looked outside to check on the weather.

"It's a great day, Murphy, there won't be a thunderstorm today. We'll take you for a run as soon as we're dressed. The constables are coming, and we're going to help them search the turret," Alice said.

Avery and Sullivan were laughing when they pulled up at the front gate. "What's so funny?" asked the twins who welcomed them.

"When your mother told us that you had found two sacks of gems with six emeralds each, we didn't believe her at first. "We're astounded.

Sullivan and I can't help but have a chuckle. You're only 11 years old. We want to know how you did it," Avery admitted.

Alice and Emma were grinning from ear to ear. "With help from our special search dog, Murphy," Alice said when everyone—Alice, Emma, Mum and the constables—marched up the staircase to the turret. "We hope the ghost of Mr. Stone will help us find the rest."

"The ghost of Mr. Stone?" said Sullivan as he turned around to look at the girls and almost tripped on the stairs. "What's that about?"

"Have you seen the ghost?" Avery asked.

"Yes," said Alice. She walked over to the desk beside the telescope with Emma who was itching to tell the constables what they had witnessed.

"Yesterday was an amazing day," began Alice, "thanks to Murphy and his little accident."

"Accident? He looks fine to me." Sullivan raised his bushy blonde eyebrows and looked at Murphy who was peacefully lying on the mat beside the doorway.

"He's okay," answered Emma. She told the constables how Murphy's accident led them to stumbling across the gems. "He was scared, that's all."

"We screamed at the top of our lungs, and Mum came running," Alice said breathlessly. "She thought something awful had happened. But, when she saw twelve sparking emeralds, she screamed too."

Emma held up the two jewel bags. "Here they are. But wait, there are more." She went to the brass bell and picked up another bag from a nearby shelf. "There are six more emeralds in here." She walked over to Avery and dropped all three sacks into his cupped hands.

"I talked Alice into opening up the macramé on the brass bell's clapper cord so we could see what the coloured thing was beneath the knots. We know we should have asked you, Mum, if that was okay, but we couldn't wait. We had to see what it was."

Alice joined Emma and looked first at her mother, then directly at the constables when she spoke. "We didn't tell Mum or Dad about this sack and cutting through some of the fancy knot work because we were in a hurry. We tried to be careful. If you look at the cord you can see most of it is still there."

The turret was quiet for a moment. No one

spoke. The twins looked remorseful, but at the same time they were anxious to get on with the search for the remaining emeralds.

"We're sorry for ruining the clapper cord. We know it's old and can't be replaced. But, we wanted to help find the emeralds quickly to end all the sad things that have gone on here," Alice said, her voice quivering. "We wouldn't have found the emeralds otherwise."

"There are three more sacks missing. Ah. I mean two," said Emma, for a moment forgetting the one she and Alice had found empty in the passageway.

"Hmm," said Avery. "What's this about two sacks missing? If there were two sacks found in the barrel and one wrapped with clapper cord, doesn't that mean that three more are still out there?"

Emma's face was expressionless. "Yes, but one was empty. So that leaves two."

Avery was impatient. "Please explain."

"Well, when we heard you were going to search the house for the missing emeralds today, we thought we could help by trying to locate them first so you wouldn't have so much work to do. Before we found the ones from the barrel in the turret," said Emma, "we searched the passageway and found a brocade sack on a tiny shelf, but it was empty. Someone had already found the gems. Maybe it was Mrs. Stone. Anyway, we put it back where we found it."

"So, that's two sacks still missing," Alice reiterated. "When we found it we didn't say anything because it was empty. We didn't think it was important."

"Okay," Avery said slowly. "Now, what about seeing the ghost? When and where did you see him?"

"When the thunderstorm rumbled through yesterday," said Emma, anxious to tell everyone that she and her sister had finally seen the ghost. "Mum and Dad were quite excited when we told them. A lot of people have seen him—Nora, Mr. McTavish, Mr. Allen and some other neighbours. It was Mr. Stone. We could tell by his white curly hair and beard." She pointed to the painting on the wall. "You have to be patient. He appears when the lightning flashes, but not every time it strikes. We stood in the rain and watched the turret as the wind spun the whale around. It was scary and chilly waiting, but worth it."

"We only saw him for a couple of seconds. He stood next to the telescope and was holding onto it with one arm, like he was trying to show us something. When we saw him, we weren't frightened. He looked right at us like he was trying to communicate. It was then that I had a hunch. I think the last two sacks of emeralds are underneath the telescope, where it's screwed down to the wooden stand," Alice said excitedly. "I think he's been trying to communicate that for a long time—standing by the telescope during a thunderstorm to let Mr. Allen and Mr. McTavish know that the emeralds were hidden there. We should search right now and see."

Their mother and the constables, flabbergasted by Alice's confidence, stood there with raised eyebrows, eyes wide, staring at the girls.

"Let's have a look, then," said Avery who looked like he and Sullivan were about to be upstaged, again.

Sullivan reached into his pocket and chuckled. "I just happen to have a little screwdriver set with me. I never know when it's going to come in handy."

It took both Avery and Sullivan several

minutes to take out the old screws, and lift the heavy telescope from its position. They laid the valuable instrument gently on the desk before returning to the telescope stand. Everyone was silent, waiting to see if the remaining gems were hidden inside.

Avery reached into the cavity and moved his hand to the bottom of the hole. He looked at the twins as he felt his way around the space.

"Is there anything there?" the twins asked, their eyes wide with anticipation.

"There is, isn't there? You found the emeralds, didn't you? You're teasing us, making us wait so long," Alice blurted.

The girls were startled when Avery suddenly let out a whoop and hoisted two little gem sacks from the telescope stand. "Yes, I found them, thanks to my favourite young sleuths, and the ghost of Mr. Stone, of course. Well done, Alice and Emma. Your intuition is commendable, Alice. You have an astonishing gift."

Avery and Sullivan shook hands with the girls who were grinning from ear to ear. "What a case this has been," Avery beamed, letting out a big sigh of relief. "This is one for the record books."

"For sure," chuckled Sullivan, "and there will never be another one like it."

"The matter of Mr. Stone's bequests, Mr. Allen's indiscretion and the burial of Mr. and Mrs. Stone's ashes, as well as Neptune's, will be finalized soon," boomed Avery. "That makes me very happy."

CHAPTER THIRTY-ONE

Rex Allen and Thomas McTavish bumped into one another outside the police station just before going in for their joint interview. Neighbours for eleven years, the pair hadn't seen one another since Mr. Allen sold his West Kings Road home and moved from the neighbourhood a few weeks earlier.

Thomas shook hands with his old friend. "Nice to see you Rex. How's it going at your new place? I miss your company and our chats over the fence."

"Good to see you too, Thomas, but I wish it were under happier circumstances," Rex replied soulfully. "I miss the old house, but it was a lot of work. I'm not as agile as I used to be. I had a lot of good times there, but some bad, which is the reason I'm here today. I had a call from Constable Avery yesterday to come in for an interview this morning.

He told me you'd be here too. Something about Rhys Stone's will that the twins found in the telescope stand of all places. I'm amazed that they found it, after all my fruitless searching for it with Caroline. I'll be glad when things are finally sorted out. I've been haunted for years about his death, and the unfinished business."

"I can remember the day clearly when he asked us over to his place to help with the document. You were appointed executor and I acted as the witness. It was in 1928 if I remember rightly. He wanted to make sure that all his emeralds were looked after when he passed on. Now the family's all gone, and we old guys are still here. Life's not fair, is it?" Thomas shook his head sadly.

"Life's a struggle sometimes, I won't argue that," Rex answered. "The sins of my past have come back to haunt me. Burying him beneath the floor in the chicken house was a dreadful thing to do. I've regretted it ever since. Every time I saw Rhys' ghost in the turret I relived the agony. Now I'll have to pay for what I did. I'm sure the police will…"

"Yes, I heard, but I know you must have done it under duress." Thomas touched his friend's arm lightly, comfortingly, not wanting him to fret anymore. "Caroline was a difficult and confused person, such a tragedy considering what a lovely woman she was before Heather died. I'm sure the authorities will take everything into consideration before making their decision. We'd better go inside. We don't want to start off our meeting on the wrong foot and be late."

"Good morning, gentlemen," said Avery when he spotted the pair walking in the front door. "You both know my partner, Constable Sullivan. Detective Lombardi is waiting for us." After being ushered into the detective's office, Mr. Allen and Mr. McTavish sat down beside the constables and tried to relax.

"I'd like to begin with Rhys Stone's will which our young sleuths, Alice and Emma Eden, found recently in the turret's telescope stand," said Lombardi and took the old document out of its envelope. "Both of you are mentioned in the will, I see. You were appointed executor, Mr. Allen, and Mr. McTavish, you acted as a witness to the document. These are your signatures. Is that correct?" the detective asked when he laid the will on his desk.

"Yes," the men answered when they peered at the long lost piece of paper.

"And that was in 1928? August 24th to be exact?"

"Yes," Mr. Allen and Mr. McTavish nodded again.

"Now it's 1951, and a lot of water has passed under the bridge since then. I understand that Mr. Stone was declared legally dead some time ago, and that some of his assets were dispersed."

"Yes," said Allen, "everything except the emerald collection and the emerald collar which Rhys' dog wore. He told me that he had hidden the emeralds in little sacks around the house, mostly in the turret and that I'd know where to find them after he died. I looked alright, but I never found them. As for the emerald collar, Thomas and I are well aware that Rhys buried Neptune, with his collar, in the garden after his pet died—it was mentioned in the will. We refrained from ever bringing the matter up because of Caroline's greed and instability, as well as Rhys' stipulation that the emerald collar was to be passed on to Nora Stevenson upon his death. We didn't want to open a can of worms."

"It was very stressful," added Mr. McTavish. "Because the will couldn't be found after Rhys disappeared, there was no point in having the dog exhumed. Besides, no one would have believed us that Rhys wanted the emerald collar to go to Nora, rather than his wife. So, we kept quiet. We found that difficult. But, now the will has been located, and Murphy led police to Neptune's burial site, it can finally be presented to Nora like Rhys wished."

"What you've told us will certainly aid in finalizing the will's bequests," advised Lombardi. "Thanks to Alice and Emma and their little dog, all the emerald sacks, except for one which was empty, were found in the turret with six emeralds in each, as described in the will. Those can be dealt with too. The empty one was located when they searched the passageway between the piano room and the sunroom. Do you know anything about the empty sack, Mr. Allen?"

"No," answered Mr. Allen. "As I've said, I never found any of the gem bags. I'm very pleased that they've finally been discovered, but I have no idea about one being empty. Honestly. I don't know what else to say."

"Mr. McTavish, I'd be pleased if you could

step out of the office for a moment. We have something else to speak to Mr. Allen about. We'll just be a couple of minutes." The old man picked up his cane, patted his friend on the shoulder, and left the room to wait in the lobby.

"About your impropriety, Mr. Allen, regarding the burial of Mr. Stone's body, everything has been taken into consideration regarding the matter. Given your previous statements, the fact that you felt coerced, and the lack of verification due to Mrs. Stone's unfortunate death, no charges will be laid," said Lombardi.

"Thank you for letting me know," said Mr. Allen. He left Lombardi's office with relief and a flood of emotions. Avery and Sullivan walked with him to the bench where Mr. McTavish sat patiently waiting for his friend.

"Thank you both for coming in," Avery said as he shook hands with the pair. "We'll talk again soon."

"How did it go, Rex?" Thomas asked.

"No charges will be laid," he answered with a sob. "I'm so grateful. Now I can get on with my life."

CHAPTER THIRTY-TWO

I t didn't take long to finish the chicken house renovation over the weekend thanks to a team effort. Nora, Lizzy and Marie not only helped Alice and Emma with the painting, but assisted their Dad by carrying boards for the floor and cedar shakes for the roof so he could spend his time nailing them all in place. Even Murphy joined in by fetching a bag of nails or a paint rag when needed. The last thing to do was give the little library a name.

"Granny always had a name for her homes," Alice told their friends. "That's popular in England where she came from. Her last home in Summerland was called "The Bank House" because it was built on the top of a hill. She chuckled and said, "It wasn't a place where you went to get money."

"We have the perfect name for the library," said Emma. "We're calling it *Rosie's Place* because Rosie used to live here."

"Who's Rosie?" Lizzy and Marie asked with a frown.

"Rosie was the name of Heather's favourite little chicken when the Stone family raised hens for their eggs," Nora told the twins' friends. "We played with Rosie when she and the other chickens were scratching around for food. During the night she roosted in the chicken coop with all the other hens. Now her home has become a library. I think *Rosie's Place* is a very fitting name."

While Nora was reminiscing, Alice and Emma found a spare shingle, penciled *Rosie's Place* on the board, and then painted the letters red. When the paint was dry they hung the sign over the doorway.

Emma stood back and admired the building. "It looks wonderful. I love it. Thank you everybody for helping us finish the library on time."

"And thanks to you, Dad for making our wish come true," said Alice. The twins were about to fetch their mother for a final tour of the place when they saw her carrying a platter of grilled cheese sandwiches down the back steps.

"Time for lunch everyone," Mum called. She walked toward the library and put the sandwiches down on a makeshift table. "I thought you'd all be hungry by now."

"Come and have a good look, Mum," said Alice. The twins took their mother's arm and showed her around the newly painted green and white library. "We even made a sign."

"I see that. I love the name you've chosen. Painting it red, the same colour as the front stairs finishes the little house off nicely. Granny would have loved it," she said, as Avery and Sullivan strolled into the back yard.

"Hello, everyone. I thought I heard voices back here," Avery called. "That's quite the reading and writing room." The constables walked over to Dad and shook his hand. "Great job. You met the deadline. The girls must be pleased to bits."

Alice and Emma beamed with excitement. "We love it," said Emma, "and can't believe it is finally finished. Lizzy and Marie helped us, and Nora, who's got longer arms than us to reach the high spots to paint." Everyone chuckled.

"Even Mum did a bit of painting, but mostly

she made us snacks and lemonade," said Alice. "Now, she's just brought out lunch. Can you stay and have a sandwich and a drink with us?"

"We'd like to, but we've got a lot of work to catch up on." Avery quickly changed his mind when he saw Nora smiling at him and the twins' disappointed faces. "I think we've got time for lemonade though, while we tell you the good news."

"What is it?" asked Alice and Emma when Lizzy and Marie ran off to play with Murphy.

"A decision regarding the finalization of Mr. Stone's assets has been made. A meeting to distribute the gems and Neptune's collar has been scheduled for 10am Tuesday at the police station. Thomas McTavish, who witnessed Rhys Stone's will, and Rex Allen, the executor, have already been notified. As you know, Mr. Allen is one of the two surviving beneficiaries, and you, Miss Stevenson, are the other," advised Avery.

"May we come?" asked the twins.

"Certainly," Avery chuckled. "You're the ones who found the will and located the emeralds. We wouldn't be having this meeting if it hadn't been for you."

The twins grinned.

"Oh, I should also mention to all of you that no charges will be laid against Mr. Allen for his part in the burial of Mr. Stone. Though I shouldn't voice my opinion about that, I have to say that I'm very pleased with the decision."

Everyone agreed that it was wonderful news. "Mr. Allen is a nice man," Nora said. "Hopefully, he'll be able to put all the sadness behind him now, with the help of his great-nieces. Children are a blessing. None of this would have been possible without Alice and Emma."

"I know we'll never have another case like it, and we'll probably never see such dedicated sleuths again," said Avery. "Thanks for the lemonade. We'll see you all on Tuesday."

CHAPTER THIRTY-THREE

We're pleased to see you all today," said Detective Lombardi when Rex Allen, Thomas McTavish, Nora Stevenson and the Edens sat down for the meeting alongside Constables Avery and Sullivan. Neptune's hand-tooled dog collar with the huge emeralds, and five bags of gems, lay on Lombardi's desk in front of them. Everyone drew in a deep breath as Lombardi untied each sack, one at a time, and emptied its contents. Thirty sparkling, precious-cut emeralds rolled across the polished surface of the wooden desk and glistened in the bright sunshine which filtered through the open slats of the venetian blinds in his office. But, none glimmered as brightly as the precious green rocks which once adorned Neptune's neck.

"They are truly beautiful," Lombardi said

before he picked up the will and read the section relating to the emerald bequeaths. "Since one of the sacks was found empty, five of the original six, filled with six emeralds each, remain as you can see. Because Mrs. Stone, named as the beneficiary of the gems, is no longer living, the thirty emeralds become the property of Mr. Allen as stipulated in the will. Neptune's emerald collar will be passed on to Miss Stevenson, according to Mr. Stone's bequest."

Alice and Emma noticed that Mr. Allen and Nora had tears in their eyes. They were moved by the proceedings too, but remained quiet as Lombardi put down the will and picked up the document that had to be signed by the beneficiaries and witnesses before the items could be distributed. After the document had been duly executed Lombardi said, "It gives me great pleasure to present you with Neptune's valuable collar, Miss Stevenson," as he placed the collar in Nora's shaky hands. "And, Mr. Allen it pleases me to hand over Mr. Stone's emerald collection to you. This has been a difficult and unusual case for our department, and we're all thrilled that it's come to a happy conclusion. Keep them in a safe place. Mr.

Stone would have been pleased to know that his will has been finalized and that the emeralds are in good hands."

Nora and Mr. Allen clutched their treasures lovingly as they expressed their thanks and shook hands with the detective and the constables. Alice and Emma couldn't help but hug them both. "We're happy for you. Now we can have the memorial service to say our final goodbyes."

CHAPTER THIRTY-FOUR

Nora and the twins were looking forward to the unusual graveside service. Nora, who had suggested the joint burial of Mr. Stone and the dog's ashes, in the first place—before Mrs. Stone's recent death—had looked after everything. A marble tombstone, engraved with the names of Heather's parents, Rhys and Caroline, and the image of Neptune, was placed next to Heather's. The delicate fragrance of the floral arrangements, carefully chosen by the twins, floated on the summer breeze and brought a feeling of calm to all who grieved.

It was a moving event led by a minister from St. Martin's Anglican Church where Heather's memorial had taken place 25 years before. The group of mourners was small, but that didn't diminish the fact that the Stones had been much loved. Everyone, in one way or another grieved the loss of the entire family.

The twins were thrilled that Constables Avery and Sullivan showed up with Detective Lombardi who, despite his off-handed demeanour, admitted that this unusual case had pulled at his heartstrings too.

"They were a family, now they're all together again," said Emma wistfully after the service. "And Neptune is with them too. That makes me happy."

"Me too," sniffled Alice as she gazed at the tranquil setting of giant evergreen trees, freshly mowed lawns, and manicured shrubbery which provided a lovely backdrop for the reverent setting of gravestones and monuments. "It's a beautiful place for them to be."

"It was a good send-off," Nora told the girls as they approached the area where a table and chairs had been set up for mourners to gather and share stories while they enjoyed a cup of tea and English pastries. "Heather would have appreciated this. She loved tea parties, just like you do."

Alice looked into Nora's kind eyes. "You're a very special friend. It would have been wonderful if we all could have been friends together. Just think of all the fun we could have had, and all the mischief we could have gotten into." The three of them laughed, happy to chase away the tears.

"I'm lucky to have such a nice family living next door to me. You've renewed my faith in fun and laughter. I've been sad for far too long. Now, let's mingle and thank the police before we have some refreshments."

As they walked toward the officers, the twins couldn't help but notice how regal they all looked in their freshly pressed police uniforms with shiny brass buttons. "I'm really going to miss them," said Alice.

Emma was pensive. "I always looked forward to their visits. Who knows? Maybe we'll be private investigators or police officers one day and can help people all the time, just like they've helped us."

"I'm sure we'll see them around," said Nora. "Look. They're all together over there. Who wants to go first?" The girls stood behind Nora and pushed her ahead of them. "Well, I guess I'm it." She laughed, and walked forward to say goodbye.

"Thank you for coming to the service today, gentlemen and for spending so much time with us to solve the mysteries. I'm happy the Stones are together now." Nora shook hands with Constable Sullivan and Detective Lombardi first, and then offered her hand to Constable Avery. "Thanks for putting up with me," she said shyly as she looked into Avery's eyes. She felt his hand press against hers. It was a warm and gentle hand, one that made her feel happy. "Maybe I'll see you again sometime, Constable Avery. But, I'd like to ask you a question before you leave. When I first met you, you introduced yourself as Constable P.J. Avery. Do you have a first name?"

"I'm Paul. Pleased to meet you, Nora," he said with a winsome smile that lit up his tanned face. "And, thank you for all your help. Your first-hand knowledge of the Stone family was paramount in solving this strange case. Next time we meet, it will be under much happier circumstances, I know.

"And, my favourite little sleuths, Alice and Emma, what can I say?" He smiled at the 11-year old twins and shook their hands. "Thanks to your investigative skills and your clever dog, Murphy, the Stone family mystery was solved. Don't forget to drop by the station and say hello sometime. If we have a difficult case, we'll know who to call, right?"

The twins giggled. "You can call us anytime. We're going to miss you."

When the police left, Alice smirked when she looked at Nora and said, "I think Constable Avery likes you."

"I think so, too," added Emma. "Maybe he'll ask you out one day."

The girls danced around Nora in their flowered summer dresses when Nora rolled her eyes at them. "That would be nice wouldn't it? Now, let's have a bite to eat before I collect the McTavishes and take them home."

When Alice and Emma found Lizzy and Marie at the refreshments table, their great-uncle, Mr. Allen, came by.

"It's nice to see the four of you together. I just had a chat with your parents, and they're thrilled with a proposal I have devised. After receiving the emerald collection I wondered what to do with the valuable gems. I'm an old man now. I don't plan on taking any trips abroad, or buying anything new. I don't really need the money. I like my little house and I'm happy now that things are settled.

"It didn't take me long to figure out what I

should do. I'm selling the emerald collection, then setting up investment plans for each of you so that you will have enough money for a good university education after you graduate from high school."

Alice, Emma, Lizzy and Marie, wide-eyed with astonishment, didn't know what to say at first, other than a heartfelt thank you. Lizzy and Marie hugged their great-uncle and Lizzy said, "That's a wonderful surprise, but won't you miss the emeralds?"

"No. I'm not fond of jewelry," he chuckled. "A good education for the four of you is much more important than valuable green gems."

"It's very kind of you, Mr. Allen, we could never thank you enough," said Alice, while Emma smiled and nodded in agreement.

"Your family has done so much for me, Alice and Emma. We wouldn't be here speaking today if it hadn't of been for you. Now, none of you will have to worry about your futures. That makes me feel good. I'm about to go home for a rest, but first I'll say goodbye to Nora, and the McTavishes. Enjoy what's left of your summer holiday."

After everybody had shared their stories and enjoyed a cup of tea and goodies, they left the cemetery. The twins lagged behind, not wanting to go home right away. "Looks like another storm is brewing," Emma said. "I see lightning over the mountains. Those black clouds are rolling in fast."

"Come on, girls, time to go," their mother called. "I'm off to join Dad. He's waiting in the car."

"Listen. It's thunder," Emma said when she and Alice turned to leave. "The storm will be here soon."

Without warning, a brilliant flash of lightning zigzagged through the sky and struck the tallest monument in the cemetery, a massive stone cross, which blew apart in an instant. A deafening crack of thunder followed as fragments of stone flew everywhere. Large pieces landed on gravestones, damaging some and obliterating engraved plaques on others. Ornamental objects were struck, and containers of flowers were smashed to bits. For a moment the twins were too frightened to move.

"Wow. That was the scariest thing I've ever seen. We're lucky it didn't strike any closer. We could have been killed," screamed Alice.

"I'm frightened. Let's go," cried Emma, who began to run.

"Wait. I hear something. It isn't thunder. It sounds like a dog whimpering," said Alice. Emma stopped in her tracks. Alice glanced back at the Stone's undamaged gravesite. "Holy smokes, Emma. There's Neptune with Mr. and Mrs. Stone and Heather," she cried as undulating images of the family floated above the gravesite. "Neptune's barking at us. I think he's telling us how happy he is."

"It's unbelievable," Emma gasped. "They're smiling at us, and Heather is waving goodbye." The twins waved their hands enthusiastically in return, and then rushed to meet their parents who were frantically calling their names and running toward them.

"Let's not tell anyone about the ghosts," said Alice. "This will be our best secret ever."

THE END

ABOUT THE AUTHOR

Inspired by her mother's love of books and command of the English language, Penelope (Penny) J. McDonald began writing stories and poems as a child. She later honed her writing skills working in the Personnel Department of the B.C. Telephone Company before marrying and raising a family. When her sons began school she enrolled at Capilano College to study writing. After one semester she sold her first article to The Vancouver Sun newspaper and credits her professor, novelist Crawford Kilian, for getting her started on a successful freelancing career.

Penny's stories and photographs have appeared in BC Outdoors, Pacific Yachting, Western Living and a myriad of other magazines across North America for more than 25 years. With hundreds of published articles and many photo covers to her credit, she has won several writing and photography awards. She enjoys mentoring others and inspiring children to read and write.

Penny is a long-time member of the North Shore Writers' Association (NSWA), having served on the executive as Secretary and Public Relations Chairman. She is a past president of the Northwest Outdoor Writers Association (NOWA) based in the United States of America.

Her first book (non-fiction), **MAHONY: A Canadian Hero** was published in 2001.

The Emerald Collar (An Eden Twins Mystery) is her first novel. The second book of the trilogy, **The Dolphin Ring**, is planned for release in 2016.

For more information please visit www.penelopejmcdonald.com.

ACKNOWLEDGMENTS

A sincere thank you to family, friends and fellow writers who have listened to me speak about my book, **The Emerald Collar (An Eden Twins Mystery)**, over the last few years. It's taken a long time to write. Writing is a lonely pursuit, but with support and encouragement from others, finishing a book can be accomplished, despite hurdles along the way. When times were tough, your understanding kept me going and it was appreciated more than you know.

Special thanks to…

My family, including my sister, Barb, and my grandchildren, Portia and Ethan, whose interest in the spunky characters kept them on edge and led to some interesting "what ifs" which pushed me past writer's block.

Deborah Sommerfeld, DVM, who kindly shared her knowledge about dog bones and Great Danes.

Michael Pacey, graphic designer, whose eagle eye was "bang on."

Martin Crosbie, author, whose popular self-publishing guidebook and kind words were appreciated during a difficult time.

Maggie Bolitho, YA author, who was there at the beginning, kindly editing and suggesting important changes which improved the story and spurred me on.

kc dyer, multi-published YA author, for sharing ideas and her talented editor with me.

Eileen Cook, prolific YA author, writing consultant and editor who edited my book with finesse and made it so much better.

Karen Bower, Karen Dodd, Carl Hunter and Cathy Scrimshaw, members of my writing critique group, who gave freely of their time when they themselves were busy writing. Their keen eyes caught many things I missed and their suggested changes were helpful.

Ares Jun, my clever cover designer, whose intuition led to the misty look on the book's front cover and the ghost in the turret, foreshadowing the mystery within.

And last, but not least, my dedicated beta readers:-

D. Paul Avery, Claudia Stockl, and the Oates

family—Carolyn, Emily and Hannah—whose ideas for character enhancement and expansion of passages improved the story.

Keava O'Brien and Maya Tomes, the youngest of the beta readers, whose boundless enthusiasm was encouraging. Voracious readers, their suggestions for improvement were insightful and their drawings of Alice, Emma and Murphy greatly appreciated.

Thanks to you all. My dream has been fulfilled!

Made in the USA
Charleston, SC
29 September 2015